THE
LAST
ACADEMY

ANNE APPLEGATE

SCHOLASTIC INC.

ISBN 978-0-545-62439-8

12 11 10 9 8 7 6 5 4 3 2 1   13 14 15 16 17 18/0

Printed in the U.S.A.   40

First Scholastic paperback printing, September 2013

Book design by Yaffa Jaskoll

When I met him at the ocean's edge, I wasn't scared. . . . The sea was black as ink under the night sky, lapping and gurgling against the dock posts, taunting me. But the water wouldn't end my life. He would. A smile flickered across his face, like he could read my thoughts.

CHAPTER 1

You couldn't pick a better night for a pool party: fire-red sunset, a breeze so hot it practically sparked as it floated across the lawn, chips and hot dogs and watermelon lined up and ready to eat.

The whole thing was my best friend's idea. Lia was exactly the kind of girl who belonged at a pool party — blond, tan, and bubbly. When we'd become friends, way back in second grade, she'd had buck teeth and I'd had a face full of freckles and long, brown hair. Now, seven years later, Lia's chompers had morphed into a thousand-watt smile. I'd stayed freckled and dork haired.

Lia loved me because I was game to go anywhere and do anything. I loved Lia because she always had something fun to do. Like this party. It was one last fling before high school started. But really, Lia planned the whole thing so

Kevin Meyers would see her in a teeny bikini. Personally, Kevin struck me as kind of a bigmouthed jerk, but being part of Lia's plots was like having a front-row seat to my own private soap opera.

As the party started, Lia made the rounds, greeting everybody with a big laugh and a hug. I hung back at the food table, checking to make sure everything was ready. Right away, I saw there was nothing to cut the cake. I dashed into the house, relieved to have something to do, and feeling kind of smug to know where the cake knife was. When I'd been in fourth grade, my parents didn't get along so great. That year, I biked the five miles from my house to Lia's practically every day. The stuff with my folks eventually evened out, but ever since, I'd more or less been adopted by Lia's family.

I grabbed the knife and went out to set it on the table.

"Go put on your suit." Lia elbowed me, frowning at my lavender skirt and white T-shirt. The basketball guys had just dropped in — about eight of them, all wearing cut-offs. Lia's other friends, Brooke and Grace, were decked out in jeans and tank tops. Lia was the only one in a swimsuit. A brand-new cherry-red bikini, and it showed off her tan perfectly.

I went over to the lawn chairs, grabbed my bag, and made an act of riffling through it. I knew what I'd find.

"I can't believe I forgot to bring it," I had to tell her a minute later. By then Lia was asking Hank from basketball which of the four city high schools he'd go to next year. The question sent a zing of excited nervousness though me. High school!

Lia rolled an unbelieving eye at me. I tried not to act guilty. I hadn't forgotten my swimsuit. It was right where I'd left it. At home. The thing was, lately I'd been . . . well, developing like a Polaroid picture. When I'd tried my suit on that afternoon, it didn't fit. My plan had been to wall-flower it up by the onion dip while Lia flirted with Kevin, who hadn't arrived yet.

"Cam . . . den," Lia whined. She adjusted her bikini and heaved a sigh. "My yellow swimsuit's in the dresser. Go put that on."

I knew the yellow suit. One-piece, old, and ugly. Lia wore it for swim meets last year.

"I'm fine," I said.

"Please," she whispered, smiling nervously as Brooke and Grace walked over. "I'm the only one in a suit. Super please?"

Lia made puppy eyes at me that were impossible to resist. So I nodded, and she hugged me, and I trudged into the house. The sliding glass door closed on Lia's laughter as the basketball guys threatened to throw each other into the pool.

When I finally found the yellow swimsuit, stuffed in the back of Lia's bedroom dresser, it was uglier than I remembered. It was even worse on, making me look like a weird fried egg, my thighs the color of the white. I spent a few minutes telling myself how nervous Lia was, waiting for her crush to show up, standing around practically naked, by herself. It wouldn't hurt me to look a little ugly for one stupid party. Then I told myself Lia would totally owe me.

On my way out, I stepped on a bag from Girl from Ipanema swimwear shop. When it crinkled under my foot, I could tell there was something in there. Slowly, I pulled it out. It was a bikini, in a bunch of different shades of green. Lia must have bought two and decided last-minute on the red. That was so completely like her. Probably, with all the craziness of getting the party together, she'd forgotten to mention it.

I held it up in the mirror. Thing was scandalous pretty. I tried it on.

I actually look good, I thought, shocked as I twisted and turned in front of the mirror. Unlike my swimsuit at home, this fit me perfectly. I mean, I didn't even look like myself. And since my other option was fried egg . . .

I walked back to the party. At the sliding glass door, I had to do a little happy dance for my BFF — Kevin had arrived. He stood with Lia, right next to the Jacuzzi. He slouched as she talked, his hands in his jeans pockets, tossing his head every few minutes to get his glossy brown hair out of his eyes.

The underwater lights for the pool were on, and the sky was twilight. Hank peeled off his shirt, cannonballed into the water, and came back up, laughing. One of his buddies dove in after, and Grace laughed. Out of nowhere, Hank caught my eye and smiled at me. Completely giddy, I sort of pranced down the path toward Lia.

"Whaddaya think?" I asked, pointing at the suit and laughing. I thought Lia'd laugh, too. Instead, Kevin let out a low whistle.

"Whoa there. Niiiii-ce," he said, checking me out. I blushed, embarrassed by his tone. I didn't know what Lia saw in him. "You are smoking hot." He grabbed my hand and spun me like we were dancing. I heard myself giggle, but I could see Lia's face going red. I was messing up her plan. Worse, I was hurting her somehow. I pulled my hand away.

"That's not the yellow suit," she said. "It's my brand-new one."

Brooke came over. "Isn't that Lia's new suit?" she asked, which made me mad, because Brooke was just saying it because Lia had said it. My best friend flashed the fakest smile I'd ever seen. It hit me like a ton of bricks: She hadn't forgotten about the green bikini at all. She'd wanted me to look ugly.

I stood there, tensed up, meeting Lia's eye. Then Kevin broke the silence.

"Whatever," he said. "This party sucks. Wanna get out of here, Camden?"

That's when Lia said, "No. She's gonna go swimming."

She smacked my chest, knocking the wind out of me. As my feet left the ground, I saw the first star, winking in the sky. And then I was in the Jacuzzi, getting water up my nose. My butt smacked the concrete seat, and I swirled down through the bubbles. Up there, they laughed at me. And right in that moment, I never wanted to be friends with Lia again.

CHAPTER 2

Five days later, I was still fuming at Lia as I packed for boarding school. She hadn't called to apologize, and I sure hadn't called her. It was totally unbelievable she was going to let me leave for California without even saying good-bye. I was throwing clothes into a duffle bag when Mom came into my room, carrying a box. She sat down on my bed. I threw a last pair of jeans in the bag and sat down next to her.

"I found some things of yours," Mom said. She handed me an old photo from my ninth birthday. It was a picture of the cake Lia had made me — homemade and lopsided, with HAPPY BIRTHDAY CAMDEN in Lia's uneven icing scrawl. As it turned out, the cake was a water balloon covered in frosting. When I'd cut it, the whole thing exploded.

I didn't touch the photo. Mom dropped it back in the

box, sighed, and pulled out an old teddy bear Dad had won for me at the fair when I was six. Downstairs, Dad was rummaging around in the kitchen. He wasn't so great with good-byes.

"How are you feeling?" Mom asked, patting my hand.

I said, "Last night, I dreamed I was standing in the doorway of an airplane. I was up in the sky, and everybody was yelling, 'Jump-jump-jump!' But I didn't have a parachute."

I knew right away I'd said the wrong thing. I could see all the energy deflate out of my mom. Like she was a vacuum and I had tripped over her cord and unplugged her from the wall. *It's just a dream*, I wanted to say. It was just a stupid dream. I had practically forgotten about it already. Nervously, I ran a hand through my newly short hair. What used to be wavy to my waist was now swinging below my chin. Good-bye, dorky, hello, new me.

Mom's eyes scanned the carpet. This meant she had lots of things to say and was shuffling through to find one she liked.

I was already enrolled. I'd signed papers and taken tests. My dad had sent a big, fat check. Somewhere out there, a girl named Tamara Stratford knew I was supposed to be her roommate, just like I knew she was supposed to be mine. I had to go. But I was scared. My parents, Lia, my old school, the small suburb of Minneapolis where I'd lived all my life — everybody and everything I knew stayed here. Only I was leaving. I could hardly breathe, I was so scared.

I wanted to crawl over and rest my head in my mom's lap. Nestle right in and listen to her heart thudding away in her chest and smell the good smell of her. But I was fourteen years old and so I just sat there with my mom, who was usually a total chatterbox, and both of us were quiet.

Then she said, "Well, Camden. You don't have to go if you really don't want to."

And that's how I knew I was going for sure.

CHAPTER 3

I love watching out the window when a plane takes off. The buildings and cars get smaller and smaller while the earth stretches out bigger and bigger. It's like looking in a fun-house mirror. My stomach stayed down there on the tarmac in that good, roller-coaster way. After a while, I fell asleep, imagining my intestines dangling down below the plane, like I was a giant jellyfish floating through the sky.

Some guy tapped me on the shoulder. The first thing I knew about him, before I even got my eyes open, was that his hand smelled clean. Like soap.

"Yeah?" I said. I could feel a cold spot on my forehead from sleeping against the window. Pretty sure I had a big, pink mark, too. The plane banked right, and the guts that I hadn't left down on the ground shifted around, still trying to figure out gravity.

Early morning sun came in through the windows on the other side of the plane. It was that supersparkly, yellow sunshine that makes you yawn and blink. I could hardly see the guy who'd tapped me. He was a dark shadow with a sun halo.

They are coming with breakfast. Would you like some? His voice was low and soft and kind of got mixed up with the thrumming of the plane, so I wasn't sure at first if I had imagined it. The plane corrected, and the sun slid across the cabin. Only then could I make out the middle-aged man in the aisle seat. The seat between us was vacant. On his tray was a plate of anonymous breakfast sandwich. Maybe it was scrambled eggs on a hoagie, but who knows. Also, he had a fruit cup. I was two feet away and it didn't smell like anything but airplane.

I shook my head and tried to go back to sleep. I heard the breakfast cart stop next to him a moment later and the man murmured. On rolled the cart.

I couldn't doze off again, though, so I gave up and opened my eyes. Middle-aged guy poked around in his bowl of fruit, herding a rogue melon square with his plastic fork. He seemed very serious about this business. I got the feeling he had been waiting for me to stop pretending to be asleep.

"Where are you going?" he asked. The plane had a layover in Denver.

"California," I told him. He nodded. "I'm going to high school out there," I added, because "California" didn't mean anything at all. I mean, not as an answer.

"You are traveling alone," he said.

"I'm going to boarding school." I was kind of irritated to have to explain myself. On the other hand, just saying, *Yeah, I'm alone*, didn't exactly strike me as an A-plus answer.

The guy stared at me and I stared at him. I know sometimes people say, "skin that looks like leather," and they mean somebody's skin is wrinkled and thick and ugly like the hide of a dead cow. But the guy's skin looked like an expensive briefcase — supple and soft and not what you see on most men in real life. Anywhere beyond the realms of Hollywood or the European yacht set, anyway.

I once watched a show about modern-day mummies. There was a girl mummy they found in South America who had skin like his — she'd been dead forty years but she mostly looked like she was sleeping. They suspected the mummifier used arsenic to preserve her. That was why she turned gold and how her cheeks and eyelids were smooth. The guy on the airplane reminded me of Mummy Girl. Like he'd been into the arsenic suntan lotion. It was kind of beautiful, I guess. I mean, if you are into expensive-luggage skin or whatever.

He seemed to be waiting for an answer.

"Huh?" I asked. Because I like to sound supersmart.

He continued to look at me. There was a lone grape in his fruit cup. When he spoke again, his voice came in and out with the drone of the airplane. "Is that where you feel you are supposed to go and what you are intended to do?"

I thought he must be a clergyman. But then I decided he wasn't. He wore an expensive-looking shirt with a narrow collar. The cuffs had real cuff links in them. Not fancy, though. Like he was the kind of guy who used cuff links with all his shirts. Maybe he had a fear of buttons or something. I don't know too much about man fashion, but he appeared increasingly weird the more I checked him out.

Suddenly, he reached across the seat and pressed his hand flat on my collarbone. I guessed if he'd had a knife, he could have cut my throat before I even moved. My brain was back there in sixty-seconds-ago land, still only suspecting the guy was odd.

His fingers slid up my neck, right under my jaw, and wrapped around my throat. Slowly, he pulled me close, his eyes steady on mine. I thought: *This crazy guy is going to kiss me!* And I just about laughed right in his face, because I'd never been kissed and that'd be one freaky story I'd have to tell if anyone asked me about my first time. I could feel my blood pumping fast under the pressure of his fingers.

He didn't kiss me. Or even come close. His hand squeezed my neck until it was a little hard to breathe. I wanted to push him away, but I couldn't move a muscle. Then he let go.

My boarding pass lay on the seat between us, next to my purse. I'd tossed it there when I put on my seat belt. But it was at a weird angle and I knew he'd moved it to read my name. He gestured in the general direction of my ticket.

"You could get off the plane in Denver. Go anywhere you want. Once you get to that school, they'll keep you under lock and key. But now? Right now you are free." He winked at me and ate the grape. It was a messed-up thing to do.

I grabbed my backpack and my improperly eyeballed boarding pass and got out of there. Or at least, I tried to. What I really did was try to stand up with the seat belt buckled. My hands were sweaty. I had to use two fingers to pull up the lock because I was holding my ticket. The guy's tray table was still down, blocking me in. He shrugged at me as if to say: *What can I do? We are prisoners of my breakfast.*

So I stood up on my seat, walked across the metal armrests, and jumped into the aisle.

Think about what I said.

I'm not sure if the guy said that or not when I brushed by him, climbing over him to get away. Or if I'd imagined it.

Some lady a few seats back huffed, all irritated by my chair-stepping lack of civility. I ran to the bathroom and locked the door behind me. A wild-eyed girl with short, dark hair stared at me from the mirror. For a good five minutes, I practiced all the things I was gonna say to that guy when I went back to my seat. He was the one who should be scared. I'd call the flight attendant if he even glanced sideways at me.

When I came back, all three seats were empty. A whiff of soap remained. I turned and peered over the top of my seat, looking for the guy. I felt like a scared gopher popping out of a hole in someone's lawn.

He was six rows behind me, talking across the aisle to a curly-haired girl. She nodded at him and laughed, flashing a pretty, gap-toothed smile. She was about my age. *He's a perv*, I decided, and flopped back down in my seat.

I did think about what the guy said, though. I wasn't going to change my plan and disappear into Denver, but I was starting a new life. No parents, no Lia, no hometown, no old school. The idea made my heart beat too fast, a sea-sick churn of excitement and apprehension and aloneness and fresh-start-ness shimmering through me one by one, making my skin goose bump. Anything could happen. Anything at all.

CHAPTER 4

California smelled like sunshine and ocean and car exhaust. A van waited outside the dinky little Nueva Vista airport. My new school's name, Lethe, was tattooed onto its side. I climbed in and slung myself into a seat, tired and ready for the journey to be over. The driver seemed to be waiting for someone else. After about fifteen minutes, he pulled away from the curb.

When the van exited the freeway, rows of orange trees blurred by on both sides, making me wonder how isolated from town my new school would be. As the orange groves gave way to foothills, the van slowed and turned into an obscure little drive, mostly hidden under the shade of scrub oaks. There was an unobtrusive sign, with THE LETHE ACADEMY in gold lettering.

Slowly, we drove under the canopy of oaks, through

the dappled light. Up and up we went, the engine whining and giving a little shudder now and then. I craned my neck to get my first glimpse of the school, but all I could see were oaks.

Then the van pulled above the tree line. Blue sky broke above us and there was a bright flash of ocean to the west. *The end of the earth*, I thought. My ride coasted to a stop.

We'd come to a small meadow cut into the hillside. The road skirted around it, as if even asphalt could be wary of a place. A rusted iron gate stood, almost hidden in the tall grass. Beyond it were half a dozen scattered old stone blocks. They looked like grave markers. A breeze blew, and the grass bent as if an invisible creature walked through it. I shivered, about to ask why we'd stopped. But the driver was only waiting for the huge wrought-iron gates at the main road to open. When they did, the van picked up speed again, and we zoomed up the last part of the hill. The creptacular little meadow slipped behind us.

If you've ever driven by a country club your parents can't afford, then you know what the Lethe Academy looked like. Green lawns sprawled, so perfectly manicured you'd expect dudes in golf carts to drive by and tee off. Instead, high school students had taken over. A group of them played Frisbee, while others lounged in the shade of olive trees that dotted the campus. Every single kid was wearing shorts, T-shirts, and flip-flops. In California, September still felt like summer. I was way overdressed in my jeans and sneakers.

Beyond the teeming front lawn, all the buildings were stucco with red-tiled roofs, their huge windows flung open. East of campus, I spotted three emerald-green sports fields, chalked dazzling white. To the north, tennis courts, and then a pool, complete with a guy jumping off the diving board. I frowned at it and looked away.

I hopped out of the van and made my way to a white table set up on the lawn. It was marked REGISTRATION. The woman manning the table glanced up at me. Next to her sat a stack of cream-colored manila envelopes.

"Hi," I said, supercool as always. "I'm Camden Fisher."

"Ah." The woman smiled and ran her finger down a row of packets, her perfect nails tapping as she went. I peeked under the table at her feet. Flip-flops. She pulled an envelope from the pile, opened it, and handed me a map.

"You are in Kelser House, third room on the south

wing." She drew a finger across the printed map of the school, down some paths, around a few buildings, to a box labeled KELSER. When I nodded that I understood, she gestured toward a large building behind her. "That's the dining hall, in case you're hungry. Lunch is on now, until two o'clock." Flowering vines crept up the stucco, making it seem like some lost civilization's cafeteria. Faintly, I smelled baking bread.

"Any questions?" she asked.

"Yeah. What's that little graveyard outside the gates?"

The woman kept smiling, but her eyebrows drew up in that minimalist, Botoxed way that's supposed to suggest concern. "Right outside the big gate? Honey, that's not a cemetery." She laughed, like I was delightful as a kitten with a ball of yarn. "That's only what's left of the original schoolhouse. Before they moved everything up here." I smiled, trying not to let on how dumb I felt. "Let me know if you need anything."

She handed me the packet and I peeked inside. *Handbook of Rules*, integrity pledge, class schedule, daily commitments, a list of books to pick up at the bookstore. I'd already read everything on their website before I'd left home, including the 129-page rule book. But I guess it didn't hurt to have a copy of my own.

Another school van parked behind me, bright-orange and neon-yellow surfboards on the roof rack. Six tan, shirtless guys tumbled out, grabbed their boards, and ran off across the lawn, barefoot and sun-bleached. I probably stared after them too long, but they don't make surfers in the Midwest. Yowza. Suddenly, I was feeling the slightest bit better about boarding school.

I thought briefly of Kevin Meyers, then shook my head and glanced at the map. Time to go. I walked until I saw glimpses of the green-blue ocean shimmering between the buildings. My stomach tightened. To my right, there was a dorm with twelve identical sets of French doors along one side. The sign said KELSER.

Inside was dark and cool, like a cave. I blinked. The place was deserted but I could hear thumping music from behind closed doors. I trailed down one hallway, found the communal bathrooms and the laundry room. There was also a glass-windowed box with an old-fashioned phone inside it, since students weren't allowed cell phones on campus.

On impulse, I darted into the phone booth and dialed home. It rang once on the other end, like a shot of adrenaline right in my heart. Home. My palms got sweaty.

A girl banged on the glass door. Startled, I jumped and dropped the phone.

"C-c-c-come on, you'll be late!" she said, laughing.

"What?" I asked, then felt bad for asking, since it had taken her so long to say the first thing. The phone was still ringing. I hung it up. Apparently, I was supposed to be somewhere.

The girl had perfect skin the color of creamed coffee, and moss-green eyes. She swung open the phone booth door. Carefully, she said, "Th-the welcome orientation's mandatory, and it s-s-starts in two minutes."

"But — my bags," I protested, gesturing to the heap at my feet.

"Leave them in the c-common room," she told me. "It's s-safe. I'm Jessie," she added, and grabbed my arm. "Let's g-go."

The orientation was held in the chapel. We filed in, past rows and rows of wooden bench pews. The whole western-facing wall of the building was stained glass. The designs were abstract, with nothing that might look like a cross or a crescent or a star anywhere. The glass was rigged on casters so the entire wall could slide open and let the breeze in. Right then it was cracked two feet open. I got the idea that right around sunset, with the light coming in, the inside of the chapel would look like a disco ball.

Jessie and I sat together. Well, technically, Jessie was sitting, but she twisted and turned, like a hyperactive puppy on a car ride.

"Nora!" she called, after a minute. She waved to a tall, frizzy-haired girl in neon-blue running shorts who was standing by the chapel doors. The girl's face lit up and she loped down the aisle toward us. Girl had legs like a gazelle and she walked like a runway model. "My roommate," Jessie said to me. Nora plopped down in the row behind us. All that grace dissipated, and she became supergawky, all kneecaps and elbows. She smiled hugely.

"I'm Nora," Nora announced.

"Camden," I answered. My palms were clammy. It had been so long since I'd needed to make new friends. I thought of Lia, then pushed the thought away. Around us, the rest of Lethe's three hundred students streamed in the doors and filled the benches. A few adults found spots, but even more stood lined against the back wall.

"Greetings, everyone," a man dressed in standard-issue teacher wear said from the chapel's stage. "Welcome, freshmen, to the Lethe Academy. I am Dr. Falzone, dean of students. To our returning upperclassmen, welcome back! I have a few announcements to make. The first formal dinner of the year is tonight. Make sure you attend." He wagged a knowing finger at a group of older boys, who laughed. Dr. Falzone gave them a wink and said to the rest of us, "If you have not done so already, your assignment for this afternoon is to read your official rule book and sign your integrity pledge. They are due at dinner. It's a point a day if they're late. If you don't know what a point is, better read your official rule book."

I'd already read, online, how points were part of the school's penalty system. You got five points for cutting a class, two points for being tardy. Each point equaled an hour of hard labor on the weekend work crew. If you got twenty points in a year, the school had grounds to expel you.

Dr. Falzone went on. "And lest anyone forget, curfew for underclassmen is ten P.M., ten thirty for seniors. That means you check in. At your curfew time. With your dorm head. In the dorms. If you do not know who your dorm head is, his or her name is listed in your information packet. Everybody got that?" He smiled, eyebrows lifted. Nobody said anything. Down came the eyebrows, and Dr. Falzone added, "The floor is now open for general announcements. Anyone?"

Some students raised their hands. Dr. Falzone called on them one at a time, and they stood to make their announcement. Lost wallet, one kid said. Student council meeting, another mentioned.

I glanced around, and spied a stone marker set into the floor at the head of the chapel. I made out the name "Kirk," along with two dates, etched into it. According to the school's website, Mr. Kirk had founded Lethe, so I guessed it was a dedication stone. While I was pondering, Jessie nudged me, her body tensing like she'd recently been electrified.

"Look at that guy. No, not now. Don't l-let him s-s-s-see you. Look! He's staring right at me." She scrunched her eyebrows at someone behind us. Jessie had super-expressive eyebrows. I turned to take a gander.

There was . . . I don't know . . . only about three-quarters of the entire school population sitting behind us. I whispered, "Who?"

She repeated the eyebrow thing, but with more energetic

twitching. No one caught my eye. I shrugged. Jessie groaned at my incompetence.

Directly behind us, a wizened old teacher in a plaid button-up shirt and red bow tie leaned forward. "Shut . . . it," he whispered. Jessie glared at me. Like it was my fault.

"Mark Elliott!" Dr. Falzone called on a student with his hand up.

The guy stood and said, "Yeah. Men's lacrosse tryouts will be on the far field Friday, three thirty. Varsity and JV."

No exaggeration: The guy making the announcement was the biggest heartbreaker I had ever seen. I guessed he was an upperclassman, definitely an athlete, with thick, sandy-blond hair and an angular face. A couple of girls giggled, and he smiled quizzically at them. It was like he didn't know he was gorgeous. "Uh, hi," he said to the gigglers, which only made them giggle more. "Bring your gear," he added, and sat down. My heart was beating faster.

When no more hands were raised, Dr. Falzone dismissed us, saying we could return to our dorms to unpack and get ready for dinner.

Everybody got up. Jessie elbowed me. Hard. "What?" I nearly yelled at her. Mr. Bow Tie gave us a displeased smirk, picked up his briefcase, and got in line to exit the chapel.

Nora stuck her tongue out at the teacher's back and then leaned toward us. "What's up, Jessie?"

"I'm not going to p-point at him!" Jessie said. Her tone implied I had asked her to stick her finger in a pot of honey and go slap a bear.

"Point at who?" Nora asked.

"Him! Right. There," Jessie practically whimpered behind her hand, eyes huge.

I searched again for her mystery guy. All I saw was a bunch of huddled adolescent butts, crammed together, moving toward the exit.

"Yeah, cute," I said, my mind still mostly on the lacrosse team hunk. "Either of you going back to the dorm?"

"Gotta go meet my advisor," Nora answered. Jessie didn't reply. She was scowling at the butts.

Back at Kelser, I managed to find the door marked with a brass "3" and the nameplates TAMARA STRATFORD and CAMDEN FISHER. Inside, my new roommate, Tamara, was curled up in her fluffy, pale pink bed. She poked her head out of her duvet burrow and gave me the once-over. I wondered if she'd missed orientation.

"'Sup," she said. She kicked her legs out from her comforter and sat up. One thin arm adjusted her pillow. She looked like a toothpick in a nest of cotton candy.

"Hi," I said back. "I'm Camden."

"Yeah, *I know*," she answered. Her hair belonged on the cover of a trashy romance novel — dark auburn, rolling curls past her shoulder blades. But her face was sharp and mousy, her brown eyes dull, and she was built like a coat hanger.

As for our room, the far end had a French door. The inside was like a weird mirror image: two twin beds, two standing wardrobes, and two small desks. My side of the reflection was completely barren. Bald mattress on a metal frame, abandoned closet. Tamara's side was cluttered, her closet so packed it didn't close, her desk covered with pencil caddies and laptop cords. It looked like she'd lived here for years already.

"Well . . ." I said into the silence. "Guess I'll get my stuff and start unpacking." I turned to the door, kind of desperate to end the awkwardness.

"Are you going to be *noisy* in here?" she demanded.

"Very," I shot back, and went to find my luggage in the common room. I couldn't tell if we were being funny or mean. When I came back with my bags, Tamara was gone.

Since I'd read ye olde rule book, I knew formal dinner was all about dressing up, guys pulling the seats out for the girls, and everybody remembering to put a cloth napkin in their laps.

And on a rotating schedule, each student was assigned to waiter duty. It was supposed to keep everybody from thinking they were too privileged or something. Basically, it meant eating early with the kitchen crew, getting a quick review on which table we'd tend, and receiving an old white coat from the kitchen's closet. Lia's mom was a caterer, so I knew the basics: Serve with your left hand, clear with your right. Anyway, that's what I was doing at the very first formal dinner of school. Doling food out to my fellow classmates. Because I am awesome lucky is why.

Each table had about ten students and one or two teachers. Nora's was the table I was serving. Seated with her was a friendly young teacher named Mr. Graham. I spotted Jessie at a table next to the kitchen, and she waved as I walked by. She wore a purple, teal, and black pouf of a dress that instantly made me feel not so ridiculous in my waiter garb, so I gave her a big smile back. After I'd done my duty of doling out roast chicken breasts and rice to a bunch of hungry, overdressed schoolmates, I stood near the wall next to another waiter — a junior named Sasha. Sasha smelled like incense and was busy inspecting her nails. She looked like she thought individuals who had achieved the title of junior shouldn't be subjected to things like being on the waitstaff, and if I brought attention to the fact that she was with a lowly freshman like me, I'd regret it. So instead, I took in the scenery.

The dining hall had a wall of large windows. The view was amazing — foothills gave way to orange groves that ended in the little town of Nueva Vista below. Beyond that, the sea. Mrs. Sibley, the headmistress, was seated at a table that was dead center in front of the windows, probably to give her the best view. A bunch of senior boys sat with her. They were joking with one another, laughing. Mrs. Sibley gave them a reluctant smile.

Mark Elliott, the guy who'd announced lacrosse try-outs, was there. He raked his sandy blond hair back with his fingers and laughed. He was supereasy to look at. Taking advantage of my waiter's coat of invisibility, I helped myself to a big, moony eyeful.

And then I saw, at the other end of the headmistress's table, the man from the airplane.

CHAPTER 5

I took a step back, bumped against the wall, and pressed flat up against it. Like part of me believed if I pushed hard enough, my body could dissolve right into the wood and plaster. Stupid. But escape to the other side was so close, you know? I mean, if not for the laws of physics and everything.

Airplane guy seemed to study the ocean view, hands folded in front of his plate.

I elbowed the girl next to me.

"Who's that at the headmistress's table?" I asked, out of the corner of my mouth.

"Umm . . . Mrs. Sibley, the headmistress?" Sasha didn't even look up from her nails, letting the dripping sarcasm do the work for her. I felt like Jessie all of the sudden. I had a crazy urge to wiggle my eyebrows. I nudged Sasha again.

"Quit it, Frosh!" Sasha threw some elbow back my way. It wasn't gentle.

"Just look and tell me!"

I knew when she saw who I was talking about, though, because she got still. In a wary tone, she said, "That's Barnaby Charon."

"What's he doing here?"

She heaved a labored sigh. "He's on the school's board of trustees, lifetime membership. All the land the school is built on belongs to him. Ditto for everything you see out those windows, all the way down to the beach. That means he pretty much owns a piece of all the teachers and students here. Even Mrs. Sibley and Dr. Falzone have to listen to what Barnaby Charon says. You do not want to draw the attention of a guy like that." She groaned. "My table's out of water."

Sasha pushed herself off the wall and shuffled away. In that same instant, Barnaby Charon turned in his chair and stared right at me.

All around, three hundred other students chatted in some parallel universe I was no longer in. I held my breath. It was like having the Great Sphinx in Egypt turn and give you the old sand eyeball.

Mrs. Sibley stood up, clinked her fork against her glass,

and thanked the waitstaff and kitchen crew. She reminded the students that classes started bright and early tomorrow, and dismissed us for the night. A thousand chair legs scraped over the wood floor, like waves crashing. The exodus swelled and rose and swallowed what I could see of Barnaby Charon.

I ducked down, like I had dropped something on the floor, and crept behind a table. It seemed like a good idea when I did it. But as the sounds in the dining hall diminished and everything got quiet, I realized that hiding wasn't a good idea at all.

The last footsteps echoed and the dining hall was silent. I could hear my own breathing, the place was so quiet. When I stood up, Barnaby Charon would be there, in the emptied dining hall, waiting for me. I knew it. I could feel his hand around my neck like a brand.

Around the corner, in the kitchen, somebody dropped a bunch of pots. It made a huge crash. I jumped to my feet before I could stop myself, screaming a little. The dining hall was deserted. I ran.

I sprinted into my room, out of breath from trying to dodge Barnaby Charon. Not that I'd seen him again. In fact, even with my eyes going everywhere at once, I hadn't glimpsed so much as the guy's shoestring. He'd disappeared.

Tamara was sprawled out on her bed again. Another girl sat at Tamara's desk.

This new girl was beautiful, in that put-together way that made you wonder if she might end up on a TV show or something.

"Hi," I said.

Tamara nodded toward her friend. "You know Brynn Laurent?"

"Hey," Brynn said to me. You could tell she was from the South right away, even hearing that one word. It came out sounding like what horses eat. She tilted the chair, balancing it on the two back legs with one of her feet on the desktop. I watched her pull the desk drawer open and play around with the junk Tamara kept there.

"Ugh. Get out of my stuff," Tamara said. Brynn smirked, took out Tamara's lip gloss, and used it.

"So where are you from?" I asked Brynn, wondering if she'd already been through my desk.

"Texas," she said, smacking her lips together.

"How's that?"

"Like a fat man on a pogo stick."

While I was trying to figure out what that meant, Brynn tossed the lip gloss back in the drawer. She knocked it shut with her foot and landed the chair's front legs.

"A fat man . . . on a pogo stick?" I asked.

"Yeah. Hot and sweaty. C'mon, Tamara." Brynn got up and walked out the doorway. I'd only known her about two minutes, but already she reminded me of Lia so much I couldn't decide if I was sad or relieved to see her go.

"Come. Back. Here." Tamara called after Brynn like she was talking, but with the volume turned all the way up.

From down the hall, Brynn replied, "They're starting a movie in the commons. Bring popcorn."

Tamara groaned and pulled herself off the bed. She went to her closet and yanked a pair of sweatpants up under her formal dinner dress, grabbed a pack of microwave popcorn, and shuffled to the door. She made it look like a huge effort.

"What. Movie?" Tamara yelled down the hall.

"Shut up!" someone suggested, from behind a closed door.

"*The Notebook*," Brynn shouted back. Tamara put on her flip-flops and disappeared out the door.

After they left, I changed into a T-shirt and yoga pants and unpacked the rest of my stuff. I hung up dresses and pants, thinking how Brynn had used Tamara's stuff. Since Brynn was so pretty I bet people didn't mind if she acted a little selfish, or helped herself to things that didn't belong to her. I'd noticed that had happened when Lia'd grown into her smile. People treated her differently, even though she was the same.

My personal jury was still out on Tamara, and I told myself I should try to make friends with her, since she was my roommate. I wasn't sure she'd make it easy, though.

The room was too quiet. I kept remembering how Barnaby Charon turned and stared me down from across the dining hall. There was nothing left to unpack. I had an urge to call home again. Or even call Lia. But it was already eight thirty, and with the time difference, everyone back home was probably sleeping.

I didn't care about the movie in the commons, so I wandered back down the hall, reading the nameplates on the doors. One of the open doors had a nameplate ripped off. The one that remained said BRYNN LAURENT. I peeked inside. Hello, trophies. They lined her shelves and cluttered the top of her wardrobe. Ribbons were pinned to a corkboard over her bed, her name in gold cursive on all of them. There was a framed photograph of her dressed in tennis whites, swinging a racket. Wild guess? Brynn was a tennis champ.

The next room belonged to JESSIE KEITA and NORA ALPERT, and that door was closed. I heard voices inside, so I knocked and opened the door right away. I wasn't into waiting to see if they wanted to talk to me.

Jessie sat on her bed, her face all blotchy from crying. Nora sat next to her. Right away, I wanted to press some cosmic rewind button and get sucked backward over the threshold, pulling the door closed behind me as I went. Nora gave me a look that said: *I will kill you if you leave after seeing Jessie this way*. Still, it took a moment to decide if I was more chicken of Jessie's crying or of Nora's retribution. I stayed. Nobody said anything.

"So . . . homesick?" I asked into the awkward silence. It seemed like a fair guess. Jessie rolled her eyes and blew her nose. Nora shook her head no. I sat down next to them. "Please don't tell me you're crying over the guy from the chapel." It was the only thing I could think to say. I couldn't imagine how she'd have guy drama already, but maybe the boy was someone she knew from back home. Then I flashed onto Mark Elliott and realized that a crush of devastating proportions could happen pretty quickly.

Jessie started laughing. Or crying. Or something

You know — little giggly sobs and nose sniffles that turned into brays and barks. Like someone rolling the radio knob back and forth between stations.

Nora and I glanced at each other, worried. I couldn't tell if Jessie was losing it or getting better. I didn't think Jessie knew, either.

"Over Skinny Butt?" I asked. I didn't even know who I was talking about. And suddenly, we were all laughing.

"Jessie doesn't even know his name!" Nora cackled. Someone farted. Jessie turned purple. All fingers zeroed in on her. Tears streamed down her face. Nora fell off the bed with a thump. I howled.

"Skin. Nee. Butt!" Nora wheezed.

"What *is* his name?" Jessie shrieked.

"There's a school roster by the dining hall, you freaks." Brynn stood in the doorway, eating popcorn. Like we were a show. A boring show. She turned to walk out.

"What?" I called after her.

"With the photos you sent in on your applications! Don't you ever look at anything?" she yelled over her shoulder.

"I d-d-d-don't think . . ." Jessie stuttered. I grabbed her arm and pulled her off the bed. She came easily, like she was the kind of girl who was used to following someone.

Brynn was back in the doorway. She had a new top on and her honey-blond hair freshly brushed. "I'm going with you," she announced. "This place is a total estrogen fest. At least at the dining hall, there's a chance of running into some guys."

Brynn was right. When we got to the dining hall, there was a poster board of all students and teachers tacked up in the front hallway. I found mine in the city of faces, the words CAMDEN FISHER, FRESHMAN, MINNESOTA, written underneath. My whole existence, boiled down to four words.

Jessie scowled at the wall. Brynn pointed out her own photo, and asked Nora where hers was. Nora had a goofy picture, with her eyes crossed and tongue sticking out. "They let you in knowing you l-l-looked like th-that?" Jessie asked.

"What? Beautiful?" Nora asked back, her puffball of dishwater-brown hair yanked back in a ponytail, neon running shorts showing off her leapfrog legs. It was weird, but

Nora's easy confidence *did* make her kind of beautiful. I liked her already.

Brynn tapped a manicured fingernail on another head shot. "Here's my sucky roommate, who decided she didn't want to come to school after all," she said.

My eyes fell on the photograph Brynn pointed to, and my head filled with tingling déjà vu weirdness. There was something about the girl in the picture. Her smile. She had a gap between her front teeth, probably like someone famous and I had simply forgotten who. The words under her photo read DREA SHAPIRO, FRESHMAN, NEW HAMPSHIRE."

A door swung open behind us, and the echo of male laughter came from the dining hall, footsteps echoing on the terra-cotta tiles.

"Well, hello, fellas!" Brynn sang, turning around fast, like we had been doing something naughty. Four upper-classmen walked by, all of them still in their formal dinner clothes, neckties undone. One of them was Mark Elliott. They slowed down and approached us.

"Hello, yourself," one of the guys said. He was tall, dark, and handsome, his teeth flashing when he added, "Brynn, right?"

She winked in response. "Beau, right?" she answered. "And who are your friends?"

"Mark, Sloan, and Carlos." Beau gestured at each guy.

"Hi," Mark Elliott said. It was hard to breathe, but I managed to not pass out, based purely on the fact that I wanted to impress the guy.

Brynn looked ready to get her flirt on, but before she could, Beau's smile went mischievous. "You ladies know what time it is?" He pointed to the big clock in the hallway. It read 9:59. Jessie gasped and bolted for the doors. We were going to be late for check-in.

We raced back to Kelser as fast as we could. Jessie and I were in the back, and tennis champ Brynn had a good lead on us, but Nora must have had a fifth gear in those legs, because she was way ahead and making it look easy. Out on the lawn, it was dark and everything smelled like mown grass and marine layer. It felt good to run.

Nora got to the doors of Kelser first. She lay into them without slowing down, arms out to push them open. Her whole body smacked against them and she crumpled like a swatted fly. I made a note to remember that the doors at

Kelser House opened *out* instead of in. Nora picked herself up and pulled the door open. We all piled in behind her, desperate to have at least one foot across the threshold, when Miss Andersen, the dorm head, saw us. I don't know how she could have missed us, though. She was right there.

Miss Andersen looked pointedly at her watch. "Get to your rooms. Now," she said, in an irritated tone. We disappeared.

My room was Tamara-free even though it was past check-in. I paced a small circle, out of breath, wondering where she could be. But half the freshmen were probably missing curfew. First days were tricky. I got changed and slipped into bed.

In the dark of my room, I let myself think again about the man from the airplane, Barnaby Charon, here at school. I remembered his hand against my collarbone, sliding up to wrap around my throat. I tried to focus instead on classes tomorrow, and what I was going to wear, and when I'd get a chance to see that cute senior guy again.

A while later, I realized my roommate was in her bed after all. I guess I must have fallen asleep. That seemed a little wonky, because my head had been completely full of thoughts. But Tamara had not been there when I came in, and yet there she was — covers pulled up around her shoulders, flip-flops on the floor in front of the bed.

"Where were you?" I was surprised to find I sounded half-asleep.

"Brynn's," Tamara said. "She's afraid of the dark."

I said, "Hey, you know anything about Barnaby Charon?"

I expected her to not know who I was talking about. I mean, he was an obscure school trustee who wasn't even a teacher. But with each second of silence that went by, I knew Tamara knew exactly who he was. After a long while, she said, "Keep him away from me." Then she yawned.

"Yeah." I felt peaceful when she said that. I could definitely relate. The last bit of stress in my stomach unclenched and I slept.

I woke up in the dark. Someone was sitting on my bed.

I froze with terror, my eyes shut, and waited for a whiff of clean soap smell so I would know for sure it was Barnaby Charon. I tried to remember all those brilliant one-liners I'd come up with while I'd hid in the airplane bathroom. *Get away! You pig! Don't touch me!* I would say all these things. Loudly. Just as soon as I was ready to open my eyes.

The thing was, nothing smelled like soap. The bed creaked. I opened my eyes.

A boy sat, his back to me, on the edge of the bed. Another boy sat on Tamara's bed. Not psycho student stranglers, I realized after a second. Only boys. Probably from our freshman class, judging from their lack of muscles and the nervous sweat hanging about them. Maybe runt sophomores.

Tamara lay on her side, her brown eyes murky in the minimal light. She and the boy on her bed whispered together. I couldn't hear too much, just the hushed breathing noises they made talking. I shut my eyes.

OK. So there were strange boys in my room. They could have been murderers, yes, but the bigger issue was that if Miss Andersen found out about them, we'd all be expelled. I'd read the rule book. Being in the room of someone of the opposite sex was a huge, steaming pile of violation. I didn't think that kind of thing had a point rating, it was so serious.

I considered sitting up and telling those guys to get lost, but I figured all it would win me was my roommate hating me. Plus, it wasn't even guaranteed to make the boys leave. What if they laughed at me and stayed? Short of shoving them out the door, I couldn't make them go without calling Miss Andersen, and there was no way I was going to get everyone, myself included, in that kind of trouble.

I made like I was rolling over in my sleep and glared at the wall for a long time, furious. It might seem like it would be hard to fall asleep with those guys there, but after a while, I did. When you don't want to be somewhere and there is no way to get your body out of the situation, your brain sometimes packs a bag and thumbs a ride anywhere it can go.

CHAPTER 6

I woke up the next morning with a bunch of angry things to say to Tamara. So naturally, she was already gone. I wore my funk of irritation like a housecoat and skulked up to the dining hall. After grabbing an apple from the breakfast spread, I went over to the hallway and studied the student-and-faculty photo montage. Something else had solidified in my mind overnight: where I'd seen Brynn's roommate before. She'd been on the plane, talking to Barnaby Charon.

At first I couldn't find her picture anywhere. I looked and looked, but the pictures were in a hodgepodge.

It was probably the stress, I told myself. I glanced at my watch. It was already 7:20 in the morning. I still had to get back down to my room, make my bed for inspection, brush my teeth, yell at Tamara for having guys in our room last night, and arrive on time for my first class. It was going to be a busy morning. I ate my apple and took my time, moving over to where Brynn had stood the night before. I closed my eyes and stuck my finger out, imagining I was poking a picture.

I opened my eyes. Not a photo under my fingertip. A name where a picture had been taken down and a thumbtack removed. DREA SHAPIRO, FRESHMAN, NEW HAMPSHIRE. I looked at that spot for a few minutes. You know. Considering.

When classes let out at three o'clock, every student had to sign up for an athletic activity. Brynn and Nora went to the real sports tryouts, competing for spots on the varsity or junior varsity teams. Then there were students like Jessie and me. I knew right away we were headed for intramural athletics: open gym, weight lifting, aerobics, free swim.

The nice thing about aerobics was that it let out at the end of the hour. That meant a little extra time for other things. For instance, Mr. Cooper, the drama teacher, had asked for volunteers to paint sets for the winter play. I'd signed up right away. Mr. Cooper was this big, tall, balding guy with a soft face and wire-rimmed glasses. He reminded me of a giant teddy bear. I like helping out, and the way Mr. Cooper had lost his briefcase in our first drama class that morning, the guy seemed like he could use all the help he could get.

But since set painting hadn't started up yet, I was free as a bird when aerobics ended that day. Jessie headed back to the dorms while I swung by the tennis courts to say hi to Brynn.

Well, *mostly* to say hi to Brynn. The girls' tennis team played in the fall, boys in the spring. So it was girls hanging around the courts. Except for this incredibly perfect senior boy I might have mentioned: Mark Elliott.

He came in from the far field with a herd of lacrosse players. But as the other boys went on toward their dorms, Mark dumped his field gear outside the tennis courts, changed his shoes, and let himself into an empty court. As the girls' team trickled away from the tennis area, he grabbed a racket and began practicing his serve. I sat down on a bench and pretended to watch Brynn finish up, but every now and then I'd sneak glances at the guy.

"Why does he practice so much?" I asked Brynn, when she came off the court. She was wearing a bridal veil of sweat. That girl was a warrior about tennis.

"Why? You like him?" she asked.

"No!" I felt myself get hot in the face. Brynn squirted

water in her mouth from a bottle, swished it around, and spit it out. I was a little grossed out. She usually seemed so . . . I dunno. Southern. It was like watching Scarlett O'Hara scratch her armpit.

"Rumor has it, Mark's brother is nationally ranked," Brynn said.

"Who's his brother?" I asked, kind of overwhelmed that there might be twice as much Elliott hotness walking around campus. Lately, I'd found myself thinking of him as "Mark-Elliott," like it was all one word. Like he was a brand name.

"Doesn't go here," Brynn said. I didn't understand. But I did know Brynn's sly smile meant she was onto me. I shut my trap. There is nothing worse than someone knowing you like somebody.

Brynn wiped her face with a towel. "His brother lives in Nueva Vista with their parents. Mark's the one who got sent away."

I felt all at once supergrateful that Brynn had told me a tidbit to add to my meager MarkElliott fact collection, and stabby with jealousy that she knew so much about him. I mean, she called him "Mark" like it was nothing.

I had a sudden, perfect vision of Mark Elliott pouring his heart out to Brynn late at night on the tennis court.

What guy could not be in love with Brynn? She always stood gracefully and smiled with the right amount of teeth showing. Her hair was always so . . . bouncy. Also, she had a restless look about her, like she would get into trouble just to amuse herself. I squirmed with embarrassment for even thinking I was cool enough to like Mark Elliott when people like Brynn roamed the earth.

"I'm bored," Brynn groaned into her water bottle, before taking a long swig.

"Umm . . . Sorry?" I said.

"I know. Let's go swimming." She waved toward the pool and added in a conspirator's whisper, "Bet Mark would join if we asked."

As soon as she said it, my lungs burned and my nose stung. I shook my head, trying to breathe normally when my body wanted to gasp for air.

"Borrrrred," Brynn argued, like it was my fault.

"I don't like the water," I managed.

She snorted her disinterest. "Whatevs. Come with me." She spun her racket in her hand, walking off. *She's so much like Lia*, I thought. Which meant Brynn would probably always be doing something exciting. I could tell by the sassy flip of her tennis racket she knew we'd be good friends. I mean, leaders need followers just as much as the other way around. But after what had happened back home, there was this splinter of anger in me. People like Lia and Brynn had a streak of selfishness in them, I understood now.

I almost didn't go. But when I glanced around, the courts were deserted. Mark Elliott pummeled a tennis ball across the way. Off in the distance, the pool glimmered like a gem. And I have to admit, I was curious to see what Brynn was up to. I followed her.

Walking in the almost-sunset light, I was struck by how beautiful campus was. Jasmine hedges grew around the buildings, so everything smelled like flowers and fresh-cut grass. Upperclassmen turned their stereo speakers out the windows on the second floor and blared music. Except it wasn't pop music like from back home. As we walked, we heard Bob Marley and Led Zeppelin. Some kid in Pilgrim Dorm played thirties-style jazz.

We walked clear across campus, past the theater and the science building. Up twenty steps and across the main lawn toward one of the boys' dorms, called Hadley House. That place was noisy, roiling with guys back from sports. Their voices echoed out the open windows. The smell of steam and sweat and shampoo floated by on the breeze. Jimi Hendrix asked if we were experienced.

I followed Brynn to the Hadley House entrance — an open-air alcove with a stairway up to the second floor. When she slowly made her way up the steps, I hesitated. Only boys were allowed up there. I craned my neck and saw guys running around, oblivious to Brynn coming up. After a moment, I took a deep breath and went up, too.

We passed a little balcony halfway up the steps. I poked my head out of it and took a deep whiff of clean air. Boys were stinky. When I looked back in, Brynn was limping.

"You OK?" I asked.

"Oh, yeah." She smiled at me, but she also wore a pained expression.

Next to the entrance of the boys' dorms was a small wooden door similar to Miss Andersen's. This one said HENRY GRAHAM on a brass plate. Brynn knocked, turned the knob, and went in.

Inside smelled like pasta cooking, and I could hear a drift of classical music. Brynn got one foot into the entrance before Mr. Graham came to the door. He looked bewildered at our intrusion. I could not believe Brynn had just walked into our teacher's private home, attached to a dorm or not.

"Sorry, Mr. Graham! I didn't think you'd hear us knock. The noise outside," Brynn said. I glanced over. She was crying a little. I don't know who was more shocked, me or Mr. Graham.

"What is it?" Mr. Graham threw a dish towel over his shoulder and reached out to help her. Brynn hobbled a tiny bit farther into the apartment. I stood at the threshold, watching. "I fell on my knee in practice. I thought it was OK, but then I twisted it funny walking up here. Do you have ice or something?"

Already Mr. Graham was doing these pantomime hand gymnastics to get us to come in and sit on his couch while he went to the kitchen and filled his dish towel with ice. Brynn leaned on me. She didn't weigh anything. I helped the big faker to the couch.

"I hear you're a big tennis star. Can't have you getting injured." Mr. Graham reemerged and handed the ice to Brynn, fretting over her like a mother hen. I tried to hide my smile.

"Thank you so much," she said. "Did we mess up your dinner?"

"No, no. Don't worry about it," he said. "Do you think you can walk?"

A timer beeped. Mr. Graham went into the kitchen and poured a pot of water into a colander in the sink. Noodles. "Or do you want me to call down and have the nurse come pick you up?" he called over his shoulder.

A couple of Hadley House guys peered into Mr. Graham's apartment. "Hey, Brynn, is that you?" one of them called. They wandered into the apartment, breezing past me like I wasn't even there. "What's up, girl? You dining with the Graham-meister tonight? Is he a righteous cook, or what?"

"How's your knee?" I asked Brynn.

"You know, I think the ice is really helping." She smiled and stretched her pretty, muscular leg out in front of her. One of the boys pulled the coffee table closer so she could rest her foot on it.

Another boy handed her a throw pillow. "Here you go. Leg OK? I hear you're a pretty good tennis player. I'm Jake, by the way." Brynn was a one-woman show, with three guys and a teacher fawning over her. Suddenly, it made me uneasy to watch Brynn bask in the attention. When I'd stumbled into Lia's spotlight, I'd paid a price. I hesitated for a moment. Then, without a word, I slipped out the door.

"Any of you want noodles?" Mr. Graham called. By that time I was at the bottom of the stairs. Brynn's tinkling laughter floated out of his apartment. I was embarrassed to bolt without saying good-bye, but I had to get out of there.

I felt better once I got outside. It had become one of those completely great evenings, when everything was purplish dark with long shadows and pink clouds out to the west. The faint smell of the sea let you know that the sky went on forever that way.

Mark Elliott was walking across the lawn toward Hadley House, his sports gear slung over his shoulder. He saw me and smiled. He was like the Cheshire Cat in the twilight with that mouth full of white, even teeth.

I tripped. I guess the good news is, I didn't eat it right there in front of the cutest guy in school. I just took a huge, swooping, pinwheeling-arm stumble before I caught myself. The not-so-great news was that I heard him laugh.

"You a tennis fan?" he asked, as he got closer. I didn't know what to say to that. Did I like tennis? Yeah, right. I liked tennis *shorts*. I liked *Mark Elliott* in tennis shorts.

"I'm friends with Brynn." I kind of said it to see what he thought about Brynn, like if he got all goofy in his face when I mentioned her. He kept walking toward me. It was hard to think with the guy getting so close. Less than three feet now. He slowed down. A foot and a half. Then he was right there.

He smelled good. Salty. I know that probably sounds gross, but the way the guy smelled was like heaven. And he was so close. I didn't feel like my right self. I had an insane urge to lean over and . . . I dunno. Lick the sweat off Mark Elliott's neck, right by his collarbone. It was shocking to think that. Shocking and super-uber fantastically unbelievably gross. It wasn't even a kiss, was the thing. It was madness to think of something like that. Insane licking madness. I bit down on my tongue.

I'd heard that the juniors who took biology had to dissect things. If you chose a frog, you had to pith the frog first. That meant you jammed a stick in its head and swirled its brain until it stopped twitching. I felt like I was getting pithed by Mark Elliott.

He was still right there. Just smiling and smelling good and waiting for me to say something. Hysteria bubbled. I had a crazy idea that I might run away screaming. That's the cool way to impress guys, I hear.

Instead, I thought about what my friends would do. Nora would be totally calm and self-assured. Brynn would say something flirty, maybe reach over and touch him. And Jessie . . . Well, I'd do the opposite of what I thought Jessie would do.

I took a deep breath. I moved closer. I flashed a smile. Mark Elliott smiled a little wider and said, "Hey, you want to . . ."

Then I said the first coherent thought that came into my brain. "I've got to go."

Mark Elliott's grin evaporated. He stepped back, adjusting the weight of all the equipment on his shoulder. He had been about to say something. To me. What? I didn't know. My face was on fire. I was pithed, all right.

So I did the only thing I could think of. I waved at him and walked off. And that's not even the whole embarrassing truth. The worst was I actually kind of ran away. Like this shoulders-clenched-trying-to-walk-in-overdrive-jog run. I couldn't bear having all these crazy thoughts with my heart beating way too fast. When I glanced back, he was gone.

The rest of the walk was the best sort of torture. I played everything back in my head. After about twenty repetitions, it morphed into something like an off-Broadway song, with all the lyrics dedicated to what a loser I was. It had a ripping chorus about how "omigod-omigod, Mark Elliott actually spoke to me!" I hummed it under my breath the whole way back.

I headed around the outside of Kelser, toward Nora

and Jessie's patio door. It was in my mind to tell them both what an idiot I'd just made of myself in front of Mark Elliott. I figured Jessie might like hearing a story where I was embarrassed over a guy.

The twilight had deepened by then, and as I walked through the near dark, I spotted Jessie and Nora sitting on their porch, bathed in the light from their room. They were deep in conversation.

As I got closer, Jessie said in a gravelly voice, ". . . bigger than life. He was always t-t-tormenting me, you know? The way big brothers do. I stuttered bad around him. He made me nervous." She paused. "We were going to a movie. I said, 'Put on your seat belt.' Except, I got stuck. I said, 'S-s-s-s-s-s,' and I couldn't get the word out. And he laughed like I'm the funniest stutterer ever and started driving. 'Put on my what?' He kept laughing, every time I tried to say it. Finally I shouted, 'I hate you!' — that came out fine. He kept mocking me, saying stuff like, 'If only I knew what you were trying to say, s-s-s-s-sis,' while I put on my own seat belt." She shuddered. "He switched lanes on a curve, and the car slid off the road."

Jessie made a terrible sound. Like she was throwing up and screaming, but with her volume turned almost all the way down so you could barely hear it. Like she was swallowing it back up before it could get out. If you've ever been around someone who's puking, you know how it can make you gag, too. That's how it felt to hear Jessie — my heart lurched like it was going to dry heave its guts out.

"The seat belt saved my life," she said. "Maybe if we hadn't been fighting, he would've put his on, too. The last thing I s-s-said to him was, 'I hate you.'"

Nora leaned forward and rubbed Jessie's arm. Then I saw Nora do a double take when she spotted me standing there in the shadows. I felt like a grave robber.

Jessie was oblivious to my presence. She went on. "I dream about it. First the car goes over. The windows shatter glass everywhere, and everything goes black. Then I'm hanging upside down from my seat belt. You know, trapped. But my brother, he's broken. He's smashed on the steering wheel. Sometimes I hear him choking, and I see bubbles in the blood that's coming out. Then my seat belt breaks and I d-d-die, too."

Nora grabbed a box of tissues for Jessie. I could feel her making sure not to look over and give me away.

Jessie laughed and blew her nose. "In the d-d-dream, the dying part is a relief. The bad p-part is being alive."

"You're OK." Nora hugged her. Jessie bawled for real

when Nora did that. I got the feeling Nora kind of said it to me, too. Maybe she knew I didn't mean to be there.

I backed away, as silent as the shadows I stood in, and when I was far enough away, I ran.

Back in the bright light of my room, I took out my homework and halfheartedly dug in, still thinking about Jessie. Poor kid, her brother dying like that. I wanted to do something nice for her. Maybe Nora and I could find out who her unknown crush, Mr. Skinny Butt, was and see if he liked Jessie back. Feeling all righteous with that decided, I focused on my assigments.

But soon I nibbled at the end of my highlighter, my Spanish reading assignment forgotten. Something didn't quite sit right as I thought about how Jessie'd wiggled her eyebrows at orientation. At the time, I'd thought she'd gone twitchy from a crush overdose. But looking back now, Jessie had seemed frantic, like it was crucial I saw who she meant. What if she wasn't mesmerized by the mysterious Mr. Skinny Butt? What if she'd been frightened?

I sat up straight, stunned. What if she'd meant Barnaby Charon?

Pure paranoia, I decided after a moment. I even laughed at myself for good measure. Except Barnaby Charon had been on campus. At least he'd been there for the formal dinner. But otherwise it was ridiculous. How would she know him, and why would she be afraid of him, even if she did know who he was? Still, it was so easy to imagine him there at the back of the chapel, in the sea of people, scaring Jessie somehow.

I did the rest of my homework with every light in the room on.

That night, when check-in was done and Tamara was sitting at her desk, reading over her homework, I said, "No more guys in our room in the middle of the night, OK?"

Tamara's mouth dropped open and the bridge of her nose squinched up. For once she didn't seem half-asleep. She looked like she was somewhere between sneezing and laughing. "What are you even talking about?" she asked.

"Come on, Tamara. I saw them. We could get in serious trouble for that kind of thing."

"I don't even know what you're saying." Tamara flew out of her chair, throwing her hands in the air as she huffed into bed. Like she thought I was crazy. Her bald-faced lying pushed me over the edge.

"One of them sat on my bed!" I yelled at her.

"No one was in our room!" Tamara shouted, jumping up.

"Shut up!" someone yelled from far away.

I stood, too. We were like two gunslingers ready to draw. After a moment, Tamara lost the standoff. Her face crumpled, and she gave me a scared glance, not at all like herself.

"Look, I don't know what you're talking about," she said, but not like she meant it. Instead, it was like she was pleading with me not to make her admit those boys had been there.

I didn't understand. I wasn't even sure Tamara understood. But it was clear I'd won. "Fine," I muttered. Uneasy relief flooded through me. She slumped onto her bed. I grabbed my toothbrush and stomped off to the bathroom. When I came back, Tamara was burrowed under her covers. Our fight hung heavy in the air, like high humidity. Nobody said anything. I crawled into bed and stared at the ceiling, unable to sleep.

CHAPTER 7

I might have won the big showdown about the presence of boys in our room, but after that, Tamara began conducting a series of guerilla attacks to even the score between us. I came back to our room once to find my dirty underwear not in my hamper, but hanging out on our patio, sunny-side up.

Yanking them down made my face burn — an admission in front of everybody that they were mine. A pack of passing sophomore boys howled with laughter. Stuff like that made it a lot easier to just spend more time in Nora and Jessie's room.

Nora had this wild confidence I totally coveted. Once, I heard these two mean girls say, "Nice hair," as they passed her. Of course, these two girls had perfect hair. Of course, Nora looked like she'd stuck her finger in a light socket.

"Nice face." Nora laughed, not a stumble in her step as she walked by. She was smart, too. If you asked her a question about a homework assignment, she would say, "Check out page ninety-five." Sure enough, you'd find a bold heading and a paragraph with the answer. The best part about her was she wasn't the type to brag about all the stuff her brain knew.

One morning, when I showed up at her room, she said, "Wanna see something cool?" It was Sunday, which meant campus was pretty much deserted. It was amazing how a boarding school could become a ghost town on the weekend. People got up early and hitched rides down to town, or they slept late.

"Sure," I said. Nora loped off without another word. I had to jog a little to keep up with those supermodel-long legs of hers. She'd already been scouted for the spring track team.

She took me to the theater. The place was a giant cavity of dark emptiness. The drama class had been rehearsing for the winter play, and a bunch of sets were scattered on the stage. I'd been helping paint them after school, so I was pretty familiar with the place. Nora got up on the stage, turned, and pointed at the lights hanging off the ceiling, about two and a half stories up from where we stood. A control room was also hidden up there.

"That's where we're going," she said.

The curtains hid a narrow doorway, and behind it, a spindly flight of stairs. We went up maybe fifty steps to a loft that overlooked the theater. A metal spotlight stood in the corner, with its head tipped down as if it were sleeping. Everything else was painted flat black. The walls sloped at strange angles, making the path cramped. I headed for the control room. Nora pulled me back. She pointed at our feet, to a square opening tucked under a domed bulge in the wall. It looked like an air duct.

"Follow me." Nora got down on her knees and crawled into the hole. The space didn't look big enough to fit her, but she disappeared. I hunched down to take a look.

The painters hadn't bothered with black paint very far into the tunnel, which went back about three feet and then made a ninety-degree turn to the left. I didn't like it, but I crawled in. My shoulders brushed each side. My body cut off the light from outside.

I was going to get stuck. The thought made my palms go clammy. No one would hear me yelling until Monday morning, most likely. I didn't know off the top of my head what the penalty was for getting caught while sneaking into a secret corridor. But I assumed it wasn't going to be a pat on the back and a big thumbs-up. When I inhaled, I swear my ribs touched the sides of the walls.

"When you feel my hands, I want you to stop, OK?" Nora sounded close. I wiggled around the corner and put my hand down on Nora's hand instead of plywood.

"OK." A tiny light came on and I saw Nora's head and shoulders. Behind her, a small room. "It's tricky here — the ground is about four feet down," she said.

I kind of birthed myself out of the tunnel and onto the floor below.

"Quiet!" Nora hissed.

We were in an unfinished space of some sort. The motif was shiny silver and pink cotton-candy insulation. Part of the floor had plywood on it; the rest was just open beams. Nora waved a penlight over a rumpled blanket and a couple of old throw pillows the color of dust.

"How'd you find this place?" I whispered.

"I was in the sound room last night and I heard voices. I came back later to explore and found it. I think other kids use it sometimes to hang out or whatever."

"What were you doing up here at night?" I asked.

Students were allowed to be in classrooms or the theater — anywhere, really — during any part of the day we weren't confined to our rooms. It wasn't like she was breaking any rules. It was just . . . weird.

"I was making out with Thatch Haskell in the sound room," Nora replied.

After a moment I managed to close my mouth. Thatch was a chunky freshman who would tell you how he was named after his infamous pirate great-great-great-something or other, and not after unsightly lawn problems. Then he would laugh and say, "You know, Blackbeard?" But mostly people only gave him a blank stare, because there was no way Thatch was more parts swashbuckler than he was lawn care.

I could not believe I was actually living in a world where guys like Thatch were making out when I was sitting in my dorm room like a dork. Sadly, the closest I'd ever come to a guy kissing me was on the airplane with Barnaby Charon, with him in the role of Señor El Creepo.

"Does Thatch know?" I gestured at . . . whatever this place was.

"Why would I tell him?" Nora scoffed, apparently insulted by the question. I didn't have an answer for that.

It seemed weird to swap spit with someone but not swap secrets. Maybe Thatch was a bad kisser.

"It's a secret room!" Nora giggle-whispered. "I had to tell someone!" She got a weird smile on her face. "I want to put a door on that passageway. With a latch and a lock."

Of all the things I guess she could have said, I didn't expect her to say that. "What about the other kids who use the place — the ones you heard last night?" I asked.

"What are they gonna do? Tell?" Nora smirked.

"They'll be mad." I was grasping at straws. I knew there was a good reason not to do what Nora was talking about, but I couldn't quite make my point.

"Mad at who? For all they'll know, the faculty boarded it up." Nora grinned at me. "I'm doing it. Are you in or out?"

"In," I said. Nora had chosen me for her secret room adventure. It was like being inducted into the Illuminati or something.

"Good, because I need your help," she said. "You work with the drama teacher, right? I want you to take his keys and make a copy of them."

I thought about it. "Why do we need the keys exactly? I mean, you're going to buy your own lock."

Nora smiled at me. "If we have those keys, we can unlock the theater and sneak in here in the middle of the night if we want to. We could bring guys up here, anything we wanted. No one could keep us out."

Why are you really doing this? I wanted to ask.

Except, there, in the darkness of that strange room, I heard it, faint, barely anything. Someone yelling Nora's name, banging on a door. *Let me in!* An icy shiver slid down my spine. I knew the sound wasn't coming from down in the theater. There was something weird about the room. The smile on Nora's face melted away, and she went green. I thought for sure she must have heard it, too.

"What was that?" I demanded.

Nora shook her head, her color seeping back. "For a minute, it looked like you had long hair. You didn't, did you?"

"Let's blow this place," I said.

"Sure." Nora made like a dog shaking off water. "But you'll do it, right? Get a copy of the keys?"

I nodded. But I didn't know if I was telling the truth or not.

CHAPTER 8

Late October brought the Santa Ana winds. Hot, dry gusts swept through campus every afternoon and into the night. They howled around the corners of buildings and raked stray leaves into tiny cyclones. It was like the ghosts of September were being cast out, wailing through campus as they left. Or like an invisible prankster blowing everybody's skirts up.

On the way to formal dinner later that Monday, the wind swirled around me, trying to nudge me off balance. I was decked out in silky black pants and a cream shell. I had even put on some makeup.

It was all for nothing, I discovered as I walked inside and checked the seating assignment. Mark Elliott was not at my table. I saw him across the room, sitting next to Brynn. We hadn't talked much since I'd bailed on her at

Mr. Graham's. When she saw me, a slow, dangerous smile crept across her red-glazed lips. She leaned over and whispered something into Mark Elliott's ear.

I waited for him to glance at me, horrified of what it would mean if he did. But he only shrugged at Brynn and went back to eating, and I crumpled into cinders of relief and disappointment. It was Brynn who smirked at me. She mouthed something that looked a lot like, *Jealous?* and winked. I couldn't tell if she was being nice with an edge . . . or mean with a grin. Putting on my game face, I smiled brightly back.

After dinner, everybody had to go listen to a pipe organist play in the chapel. According to the program, the music was supposed to be "uplifting and hopeful." But I wasn't sitting anywhere near Mark Elliott or Jessie and Nora, so the only thing I hoped for was the end of the presentation. Instead, the organist went fifteen minutes over schedule. It was all I could do not to groan out loud and slip off the pew onto the floor.

By the time we were excused, the last remnants of the sunset were inky black clouds whipping across a fiery orange sky. Grit got in my eyes as I walked out the door. What a waste of makeup. What a waste of a secret room where I could go kiss someone. I was going to be a dateless wonder the rest of my life.

As I trudged back to the dorms, Nora linked her arm through mine. "I got the lock and hinges yesterday in town. Wanna come to my room and see?" she whispered.

"Sure." I sighed. Jessie caught up with us and linked arms with Nora. The wind howled and Nora laughed, happy.

She gave me a quick, warning look, so I knew we couldn't go check out the hardware after all — she hadn't told Jessie about our secret. So I said, "You guys wanna come to my room?" We hardly ever went there, because Tamara and I were still in a barely civil standoff. Punctuated with occasional swearing and unfulfilled urges on my part to scrub a toilet or two with her toothbrush.

I started to knock on my own door when we got back, but I stopped myself: Tamara waltzed in unannounced when I was changing, when I was two inches from the mirror checking for zits, and when I was trying to sleep. I didn't see why I should give her the courtesy. So I walked in without knocking.

Tamara, Brynn, and Sasha the junior were hunched over my desk, doing something. They froze like three raccoons caught raiding a trash can.

My guts went sour.

"Hey, guys, what are you doing?" Nora asked, her voice too perky and loud.

"Don't tell them. They're lame," Tamara told Brynn, in a laughing kind of way that didn't feel like a joke. They were on my side of the room, using my desk, in my personal space. I never went through Tamara's things. And what had Tamara just said about being lame?

"Get out of my stuff," I said.

Not one of them moved. Tamara smiled a huge, sharky smile. All of the sudden, I couldn't breathe. Lia had smiled like that right before she'd pushed me into the Jacuzzi. *And then they'd all laughed at me.* Thinking that, I saw red. I'm not even kidding. I'm surprised I didn't blow a blood vessel right there. I couldn't let that happen to me again.

I made the space between me and her disappear. Tamara and Brynn leaned together, blocking whatever was on my desk.

"Beat it." My roommate rolled her eyes, smirking at her friends like I was a big, stupid joke. "We're busy."

There was no way I was getting kicked out of my own room.

I heard someone say, "Wow. I bet Miss Andersen could

figure out whose desk this is, you snot waffle. Why don't I call her in to sort it out?"

Turns out it was me talking.

That's about when everything stopped and everybody gawked at me. Brynn took a small step away from Tamara. Their shoulders parted. There was a cardboard game box on my desk.

Sasha said, "Oh, take a pill. It's my stuff. Tamara's desk was covered in junk." She picked up the box and shoved it under her arm. It was a Ouija board.

Sure enough, Tamara's desk was covered with a diorama she was doing for English. Homework was scattered all over her bed. Every possible surface on Tamara's side of the room was occupied. I got a sinking feeling in my gut.

"Did you call me a . . . snot waffle?" Tamara asked. Nobody paid attention to her.

"What's that?" Jessie gawked at the game box. Me, too. I'd heard about Ouija boards before, but never actually seen one. *Speak with the Spirit World!* was written on the front. Disembodied hands floated above a wooden board, fingers touching a plastic triangle. The board had an alphabet and numbers on it, and also symbols and words like "yes," "no," and "farewell." It looked spooky.

Brynn smiled at us, eyes sparkling. "Mr. Kirk is buried under the chapel, y'all — you've seen the memorial plaque, right?"

It seemed entirely likely and also completely unbelievable that the school's founder could be buried under our feet where we just listened to an hour of boring pipe organ music. Outside, the wind scraped around the corners of the dorms, howling and whistling before dying down again.

That's when everything started to happen fast.

"When are you going?" Nora asked. Jessie added, "Where are you going?"

"Don't tell them," Tamara said. "You heard — they squeal."

My face felt hot. I was a squealer now?

"That wasn't me," Jessie said. "*I* don't squeal. You can tell me."

"We're sneaking out," Sasha said. "Two A.M. in the chapel. We're doing a séance over his grave."

"Don't they lock that place up at night?" I asked.

"Shut up, squealer. You're not invited." Tamara tossed her beautiful hair.

Sasha considered me for a moment. "You stay here and protect your precious desk, Frosh."

"I'm going with you," Jessie said. We all stared at her, shocked. Jessie never broke the rules. And she didn't hang out with upperclassmen.

"Why would you think you can go? I don't even know who you are," Sasha said coolly to Jessie.

"You're gonna let me use that board because I've got someone I want to talk to. Someone I can't call on the phone." Jessie didn't stutter at all.

Sasha tapped a finger on the box, like she was considering. "Who?"

"My brother."

"When?"

"Over the summer."

Jessie's eyes were shiny and red. Her hands were fists, and her body leaned forward, like an angry dog on a tight leash. My stomach twisted as I remembered overhearing Jessie's confession. She must've wanted to change those last words to him enough to try something crazy. Finding out her brother had died only a few months ago made it way worse, somehow.

Lia'd told me once that you could use a Ouija board to invite the dead to talk to you. But when you rolled out the welcome mat, she claimed you didn't know who was going to show up. Maybe you got a lonely old grandma ghost who only wanted someone to talk to. Or maybe you got something that would pretend to be a small child but was really a demon. And you might be able to call them, but that didn't mean you could make them leave. If you believed in Ouija boards and spirits and that sort of thing, she said. I didn't. But I didn't *not* believe, either.

Sasha nodded. "All right. You can come." Jessie's lips curled up like she was making a smile, but she didn't look happy. "We meet at the bushes by the back entrance to the chapel. Two A.M. If you get caught, you're on your own. Bring a blanket." She pointed two fingers — her index and middle in a witch's fork — toward me and Nora. "Not you two. Just her."

Sasha lowered a finger so that I was the only one she continued to point at. "And if we get busted, I'm going to know it was you. And the last thing I do before I get expelled? Is get up during announcements and tell every-body that you were the one who ratted us out. You'll never have a friend here again. Don't think I won't do it, either, squealer."

I stood there, shaking and silent. I was completely humiliated. How had things gotten so messed up so fast?

"What about me?" Nora asked.

"What about you?" Sasha replied. She threw her coat over the Ouija board and tromped out of our room.

"Come on, Brynn," Tamara said. Brynn gave me a small smile and left with Tamara.

You knew Brynn was like that, I told myself, angry that it stung so bad. *She'll go wherever the fun is.*

When they were gone, I said, "I'm sorry about your brother." Jessie was still standing there, straining against her invisible leash. "Hey, don't go, all right?" I added, taking a deep breath to calm down my shakes. "Those girls are stupid. I mean, can you imagine? Running across campus in the middle of the night? They'll probably all get caught. And come on. Did you see that board they had? It was from Parker Brothers. Those guys make Monopoly."

Jessie didn't look at me. I reached out and touched her arm. She jerked away. Tears spilled down her cheeks. "Leave me alone," she whispered, and ran out.

Nora shrugged at me in half an apology as she turned to go. Jessie was her roommate. Nora had to make sure she was OK. Then I was alone.

Stupid jerk roommate. Stupid Brynn. Stupid school. I hated everything, the whole campus, all of Nueva Vista. Throw in the whole state of California for good measure.

On impulse, I dashed out of my room to the dorm phone and shut the booth's door behind me. I meant to call home, but it was Lia's number I dialed. I don't think I even realized my mistake until she picked up.

"Hello?" she said, like she'd done a hundred thousand times before. My heart lurched. I missed Lia like crazy, but I didn't trust her anymore. And the truth was, I couldn't bear to tell her what had happened and risk her laughing at me, too. Instead, I covered the mouthpiece so she wouldn't hear me cry, and listened to her breathe until she hung up.

CHAPTER 9

When Tamara came back to our room right before ten o'clock check-in, I was already in bed. We both pretended I was asleep. She set her alarm, and I sincerely hoped it was for 7 the next morning and not 2 A.M. What if someone heard her alarm go off in the middle of the night? If she was going to be that dumb, she'd get caught. Then tomorrow or the next day, Sasha would make an announcement that featured me prominently in the role of Tattletale McSquealerpants.

I was still awake at one thirty when Tamara's bedsprings creaked. I heard her feet on the floor, and then the patio doors opened. I was so mad at her; I hoped she got caught. I was scared to death she'd get caught.

I was alone in our room. She had really done it.

My insides pretzeled when I thought about how the

consequences were out of my hands. In the dark, every creak in the dorm was a teacher coming to check Tamara's empty bed. Every gust of wind was more teachers, probably holding lit torches and the leashes of growling bloodhounds, on the trail after Jessie and Sasha and Tamara and Brynn. As I lay there, I could actually see Sasha, caught and crying. But also penning her announcement for tomorrow morning. Behind her, the headmistress called an emergency disciplinary committee together, still wearing her bathrobe.

About a minute later, it was three in the morning. I couldn't stand it anymore. I slunk out of bed and got dressed, convinced I was getting stupider by the second to do what I was thinking about doing. The patio doors opened like a thunder crack. I waited either to have a coronary or for Miss Andersen to walk in and bust me. Who could have slept through that noise?

The moon was out. Billowy silver clouds blew fast across the sky. All the lights around campus were dimmed for the night, leaving little pools of amber splashed around the pathways. I shivered.

And then I was outside. An expulsionary offense. My shoes scuffed the patio, loud as a jackhammer, so I slipped them off. The ground was cold and wet, but I didn't care. Bare feet didn't make noise. I took off at a jog, not bothering to crouch in the shadows or anything. If someone saw me, that was just my bad luck.

The crazy thing was how great it felt to be outside in the middle of the night. The air seemed superoxygenated; every inhale made me light-headed with all the energy in it. I ran, hardly needing to breathe at all. It felt like I was the only person left on earth.

But once I got to the back door of the chapel, I didn't know what to do. I heard a noise and peeked around the corner of the building.

There was nothing but scraggly bushes, a narrow dirt path, and the edge of the mesa. I could see right away that the stained-glass wall was open a bit. And a girl was crouched outside the chapel, peeking in. Candlelight from inside flickered on the stained glass, striping the girl's face with red and orange.

The girl looked at me, eyes wide, finger over her lips to warn me not to shout out. I crept over to her. It was Rachel, from my Spanish class — she was a loud, exuberant girl with pink cheeks and big brown eyes. In class, she always cracked jokes using our vocab words, and whenever she raised her hand, the teacher always sighed before he said, "Yes, Rachel."

"Are they still doing the séance?" I whispered, wanting her to know that I knew what was going on, that I had some kind of right to be there, too.

Rachel nodded. Looking inside the chapel was like seeing into another world. Everything seemed calm. The warm honey of the wooden pews and the flicker of candle-light. A blanket lay in the aisle, and the low murmurs of girls talking wafted out. From where I stood, only their legs were visible. It gave me the shivers. It was like I was spying on something holy. I shook the idea off — I'd had enough of feeling like an outsider.

"How'd you hear about it?" I asked Rachel.

"Big Mouth Sasha," she said. "She was bragging about doing this yesterday at lunch. You didn't get invited, either, huh?"

I shook my head. "They think they're so cool."

I glanced back inside the chapel, kind of grinning despite myself. All of the sudden, I had a new friend. One who thought Sasha was a big mouth. I kept thinking: *We've snuck out!* And it made me feel giddy and light-headed. I never broke rules at home. I'd never had any place to sneak out to. Even Lia hadn't ever done anything like this. It was a little hard to breathe when I actually stopped to consider what was happening. If it wasn't for all the oxygen-saturated air, I probably would have passed out right there.

Soon, the girls would be done with their séance. When that happened, Rachel and I would have to slink back to our dorms and hope we didn't get caught — either by teachers or by the cool kids. All this anger at Sasha, Tamara, Brynn, and even Jessie, came boiling up in me. I wasn't going to let them be happy inside and make me feel like a loser outside.

I studied the stained glass and how loose it was in the runner. I mimed to Rachel that I was going to shake it. Then I pointed into the chapel and the girls inside. After a moment, Rachel gave me a sly thumbs-up. I whispered, "On three!"

We were going to give them a show, all right. After all, that's what they came to see. Rachel snuck over to the far end of the sliding glass. She put her palms flat. I moved to the other end and put my hands up on the windows, too. From my new position, I saw Jessie kneeling on the floor of the chapel, head bowed in concentration. Her fingers moved slowly over the Ouija board. For a second, our plan seemed like a bad idea, and I hesitated.

But I couldn't stop. Giggles fizzed up inside me until the pressure of them was unbearable, like I was a soda bottle someone shook up and left capped. Candles flickered inside the chapel. I mouthed: *One . . . Two . . . Three!*

We shoved the glass. Hard. It made a terrific rattle, from the floor all the way up to the sliders on the ceiling. *Whap! Whap! Whap!* It was hard not to laugh and shriek. Our bottle caps popped right off. We were giving them their ghost, was all. And that ghost was an earth-to-heavens racket in the dead of night, when we were supposed to be tucked into our own beds.

Brynn screamed. Glass shattered. I caught a glimpse of Jessie's face — her mouth a dark circle of surprise. Suddenly scared, I stumbled back and saw it — a pane of glass had fallen out of the wall.

Run! Rachel mouthed, barreling toward me. Then we were scrambling around the corner and sprinting away. It was a lot better than slinking, I can tell you that. A-million-stars-exploding-in-my-chest better.

I looked back when we split off in different directions, Rachel waving cheerfully at me as she tore off. No one came out of the chapel. It was completely dark. All the candles were blown out.

Right before dawn, Tamara snuck back into our room. I'd crawled into the safety of my own bed around three fifteen and giggled for half an hour, waiting for her to creep in. Around 4 A.M., I got concerned. By the time she actually showed, I was completely sure we'd all end up in disciplinary committees by second period.

She sank onto her bed, silent. I closed my eyes and got about three minutes of peace before Tamara started crying. My own body chemistry practically electrocuted me with adrenaline. It made my heart cramp and my fingertips tingle. *They'd been caught after all.* I sat up in bed, all stiff like a zombie. Tamara sat on her bed, dressed in sweats and sneakers. It seemed weird that she didn't even take her shoes off. Her legs were tucked up crisscross. She hugged her pillow.

"What's wrong?" I whispered. Sure, I had spent all night pretty much hating Tamara. But right then? She was a genuine, staring-into-space, red-eyed mess. She didn't answer my question. So I crept over and grabbed a box of Kleenex off her desk. Nothing. I sat next to her, pulled a tissue out of the box, and held it up to her face.

Then I got it. Tamara was crying because Rachel and I had scared the snot out of her when we shook the chapel wall. I bit my lip so I wouldn't smile. Tamara sniffled. I knew if I laughed, Tamara would probably rage out. On the other hand, at least I had a working relationship with Tamara's rage face. This glassy-eyed disaster of a girl scared me.

"Hey." I gave her a quick squeeze. "Chill out. We pranked you, is all. We shook the chapel wall. We got you good, huh?" I gave her an elbow, grinned, and waited for her to get furious.

"I wasn't in the chapel. I was with Shane," Tamara said.

The giggles inside me dropped like flies. And, yeah, the feeling was as gross as it sounds. "What?" I asked. "With who?"

"A sophomore. Shane," she said. I didn't know who she was talking about. Then after a minute, I kind of did. There was a pack of sophomore guys who roved campus. They constantly punched each other in the arms, or flicked each other on the backs of their ears. I'd heard they hazed the younger boys by duct taping their ankles together and hanging them, upside down, in their own closets. Bullies. I was pretty sure one of them was named Shane.

I remembered back home, when Grace — who was more Lia's friend, but sort of mine, too — had invited Lia, Brooke, and me to a sleepover. In the dark of night, Grace had confessed how she'd kissed her chemistry partner at his house one day after school. We'd squealed with laughter and peppered her with questions: *Was it fun? What did he say? Would you ever do it again?* It didn't seem like any of these were good questions now.

"What happened? Are you OK . . . ?" I stopped.

Tamara shrugged. "Kinda," she said. "He was with Sasha when I got to the chapel. I didn't want to go to that stupid séance thing, so we ditched."

"Where did you go?"

Another shrug. "Little Quad Lawn. At first it was pretty fun. We started kissing. But then he wanted to go further. And when I wouldn't . . . he called me names . . . and ditched me." She had to take three big, watery breaths to get it all out there.

I thought of that place, and how open and exposed it was. The school nurse asleep in her cottage fifty feet away. Dumpsters on a concrete slab nearby. Not exactly Romance City. And then to have the guy call you names and bail? I felt bad for Tamara.

She hugged me and bawled for real then. I wanted to be sympathetic, but also? She smelled bad. Probably what making out with Shane next to the Dumpsters smelled like. But I let her hug me, anyway.

It must have been the stress and the lack of sleep and everything, but the odor on Tamara started to make me queasy. My ears started ringing. It kept getting worse, until it sounded like a truck backing up in my head. I thought I was going to throw up or pass out, and the whole time, she was still crying.

I thought: *Tamara's poisoning me.* It was a crazy idea, but as soon as I thought it, it felt exactly right. My hands got cold and shaky. She blew her nose and rested her head on my shoulder.

I started to feel like I was in one of those movies where someone gets radiation poisoning, right before their skin starts to slough off and their eyes bleed. My blood pressure fell through my toes. I thought, *I'm dying.* Which was crazy. I kept trying to breathe, but no air got in.

Panicked, I shoved her away and bounced off her bed. My legs wobbled, my knees trying to buckle. And then I had a hallucination.

My roommate's skin got all withered and yellowed. Her eyes turned milky and rolled up in their sockets.

Scabbed-up lips stretched across her teeth. It was worse than seeing a corpse, because she was still alive somewhere inside there. *She's the Golden Mummy Girl.*

I heard my own voice say, "He sounds like a loser. Good riddance, right?"

Then it was normal old Tamara sitting there. Except something in her eyes let me know she was still the Golden Mummy Girl underneath. It was a certifiably unhinged thought. I stumbled and caught myself. I was going to completely lose it. Freak out or start laughing until the school nurse came and shot me full of horse tranquilizers. Then the tiny boss in my head pulled some kind of switch I didn't even know I had. It shut the crazy thinking down, but it hurt my brain to have it happen.

"*You're* calling *him* a loser?" Tamara laughed. She straightened her spine and tossed her head. "You don't know anything. I'm not surprised. You're too ugly to get noticed on this campus, anyway."

A minute ago, I had been wiping her nose for her. Now any hope for becoming friends lay like broken shards of glass between us. Honestly, any hopes of me not seeing her as the Cryptkeeper was a bad bet.

"You know why you're here, loser?" she asked. My

mouth dropped open, but no sound came out. "Your parents don't love you. You're here because they didn't want you anymore."

"What?" I stumbled back. Dawn was breaking and the room was getting lighter now, by little shades of sunlight each few minutes. I could see Tamara growing a shadow. It looked like rage.

"You got sent to boarding school because your parents didn't want you. Right now your family is sitting at breakfast in your old home, and they don't miss you at all. Their life is better without you."

"That's not true." I was afraid to turn my back on her. Now it was clear what was going on: Tamara was the one who was crazy, so insane it made me sick. I backed toward the doors.

"You're here. I'm here. We're all here. Go ask your friend Barnaby Charon why," she yelled. "You go ask him why your parents sent you to a place like this."

I bumped against the patio doors, knocking them open, and ran out in my pajamas. Everything was gilded in the dawn sun. The lawn and the buildings and even the sidewalks glinted gold. But all the superoxygenated air had burned off with the dew. This new air was too thin and I couldn't breathe.

CHAPTER 10

I started keeping to myself. I did homework during announcements instead of talking to anyone in the seats near me. I went up to the lacrosse field and watched boys scrimmage instead of going to see Brynn play tennis. I brought a textbook to the dining hall and sat alone. After, I'd go to the library.

I needed the time to think. My roommate hated me. A junior had branded me as a rat and I'd broken a pretty serious school rule. Plus, I couldn't ignore the fact that I had seen, heard, and thought things that seemed pretty mentally unbalanced. It was a lot to process.

But what kept coming back to stick in my mind was what Tamara had said about my parents not wanting me anymore. I mean, I knew it was a lie. But I couldn't let it go.

Why *had* they sent me to boarding school? I'd been a good student, never the kind of kid who needed a strict, away-from-home kind of environment. It was weird, but now that I was here, I could barely remember the summer, when the decision had been made. Had I been so consumed by my issues with Lia, my life, and my friends that I'd somehow missed something bad happening between me and my parents?

Wondering about it made me feel like I was some stupid dog a family didn't want anymore and so they drove out to the woods and let it go. The family tells themselves the dog is going to be all happy chasing rabbits and frolicking and stuff. The dog doesn't even know what's going on until the car is out of sight.

Half a dozen times, I picked up the phone in the dorm hallway to call my parents and disprove my roommate's rattlesnake-mean theory. But there was always a good reason not to dial. Like I had work to do, or someone else was already on the phone, or the two-hour time change made it too late to call there. Keeping busy seemed a lot easier than having to dial home and ask whoever picked up on the other end why I was far away when they were together.

And even all that was better than thinking about those other things that had happened: The Golden Mummy Girl Tamara had turned into, or that smell on her that made me think I was being poisoned. Or what Tamara had said at the end: *Go ask your friend Barnaby Charon.*

A few days later, I sat on a bleacher seat, pretending to watch lacrosse. I felt nice and invisible there. The boys in the bleachers watched the game and the other girls mooned over the players, so there wasn't too much pressure to talk to anyone. This time, a few of the varsity players stayed to watch the JV team practice. That meant I got to peek at Mark Elliott for a whole hour. I didn't want to care about boys anymore, but even as Eeyored out as I felt, I couldn't entirely ignore him.

When the practice finished and everybody started heading back to campus, he caught up and walked next to me.

"Hi," he said. Just like that.

"Hi," I said. He was still sweaty and dirty from practice, and he scrubbed his face with his jersey. When it pulled up, I saw his stomach was completely flat, except for these muscles that flexed when he moved. It made me a little dizzy.

"Some scrimmage," he said, into the jersey.

"Yeah." I kept sneaking glances. It was like being exposed to some superprivate thing. Like his belly button was the page of a diary. "I thought Kirby was going to tank when he got the ball, but he held in there. Janson's got a serious tackle."

I had no idea what he was talking about. Game something. I nodded. When was the last time I had taken a breath? I felt kind of faint. When I inhaled, everything smelled overwhelming: the sun on the grass. The occasional whiff of Mark Elliott. My own hair blowing around, getting caught in the corner of my mouth.

"Yeah," I said.

"You know Beau?" Mark Elliott asked. Beau was one of his friends. They played lacrosse together. Beau was walking a distance behind us, talking to three other senior jocks, his hands tucked casually into his waistband, I guess for lack of pockets.

"Think you might want to go out with him sometime?" Mark Elliott asked me, staring out across the field, not meeting my eye. His eyebrows squinched together like he was angry.

"What?" I stopped moving. Breathing, talking, and walking were all I could handle. Throw thinking into the mix, and I had to give something up.

"He's kind of shy, but he thinks you're cute," Mark Elliott said, still looking off at the horizon like he was too annoyed with me to make eye contact.

I glanced back at Beau. He and his friends had stopped, too. Beau was cute. He was popular and seemed nice enough. I was superflattered, but I didn't go all flushed and giggly at the idea of him. I mean, zero sparks. He wasn't Mark Elliott, was all. We started walking again.

"No, thanks. I mean, I like him fine. But I don't . . . he's not . . ." I stopped, totally flustered. Was I actually rejecting a date with a good-looking senior? Did I just say no to something Mark Elliott asked me? How could I be more wrong?

"He's not what?" he persisted.

"I like you." As soon as it was out of my mouth, I smacked my hand to my lips, trying to grab the words back before they got heard.

"Oh," Mark Elliott said. He stopped. I kept walking. I don't know why. I just kept walking. I wanted to die.

I continued to want to die all the way across the soccer field and the baseball diamond, past the pool and the tennis courts, along the theater, and down to Kelser House.

Nora stood outside my room, pounding the patio doors with her fist. I was glad to see her, to really talk to someone for the first time since I had fought with Tamara. At least, until Nora turned around. Her face was pale and worried. I stopped. Nora never worried about anything. When she saw me, she gave me half a smile and rushed over. Compared to her usual bounding stride, rushed walking made her look pinched and weird.

"Hey, you snag those keys yet?" Nora asked, peering over my shoulder.

At first I didn't even know what she was talking about. Then I remembered her plan to lock up the secret room.

"No. What's up? How you been?"

I was kind of shocked by how she deflated, like she'd been counting on me having something I had completely forgotten about. It made me squirmy. I still wasn't sure about the whole thing — she was asking me to do something that might get me kicked out if we got caught. Then she wiped the look off her face, leaving nothing but deter-mination there.

"Come with me." Nora grabbed my wrist and led me over to her and Jessie's patio. She gave a quick, obligatory knock and yanked the door open.

The room was dark. I stood there, waiting for my eyes to adjust. Jessie was slumped on the bed, like a battered piece of luggage forgotten on a claims carousel. Her pretty green eyes, unfocused. I thought: *Just like Tamara-poison-Golden-Mummy-Girl. What's wrong with everybody?*

"Jessie?"

Her rib cage expanded as she breathed, but that was it for movement.

"She's been like that all day now. Even yesterday it wasn't this bad." Nora sounded somewhere between annoyed and concerned.

"Tell Miss Andersen." I said it out of the corner of my mouth, because it felt weird to be talking about Jessie when she was right there.

"Jessie said not to. She's been practically comatose since that séance. But last night, she would at least talk to me. Now nothing." Nora reached over and poked Jessie with one finger. No response. Nora frowned at me like Jessie was a weird bug she had never seen before.

"The séance?" I asked. That felt like a million years ago. And then I knew.

I'd been focused on scaring Tamara, not even considering how I might have frightened someone I actually liked. My insides sank. Jessie had been in that chapel, waiting for a sign from the dead. And now she was sitting in front of me like she'd swallowed cement.

I got down on my knees so I could see her face. "Jessie, it was me. I knocked on the chapel wall. As a joke. I didn't mean to scare you." Behind us, Nora took the opportunity to kick me in my butt. I didn't care.

Jessie's eyes cleared and she saw me. "Everything shook, the glass broke, and the lights went out. I wasn't in the chapel, I was in that car."

"No. We just . . ." I thought: *Why get Rachel in trouble?* "I shook the stained-glass wall. That's what the noise was." I cringed, remembering the sound of shattering glass, seeing Jessie again in my head, her mouth open in surprise.

She reached out so slowly I didn't know what she was

going to do until she grabbed the collar of my T-shirt and twisted it around her fist. She pulled me close.

"My brother told me things. Good, terrible things. You brought him . . . thank you." She stared past me, like she was speaking to someone else behind me. Dread prickled its way up my spine. What had I done?

I put my hand on Jessie's fist. We were practically nose to nose. I could smell her, but she didn't smell like poison or anything. Just like she hadn't showered in a couple of days.

"It was only a prank," I said.

She let go of my shirt and smiled weirdly. "It *was* my brother. No one could know that stuff except him."

Jessie hadn't stuttered once. I glanced up at Nora. She looked at me with one eyebrow raised.

"Umm. Ohh . . . kay. What did your brother say?" Nora asked.

Jessie shook her head and mashed her lips together until they were nothing but a white crease. Then she muttered into the front of her shirt, "He told me he was sorry, that it wasn't my fault. He told me I could go home if I wanted to."

"You want to go home?" I wondered how come no one besides Nora had noticed what had happened to Jessie.

Except I hadn't noticed, and she sat right next to me in the chapel every day.

Jessie shook her head, that thin scar for a mouth coming back. "My parents don't want me back. I look just like him." She glanced at her desk. It was fairly neat — one textbook, some papers, a strange little gold coin, and a framed photo of Jessie, with her arm around a tall guy with the same moss-green eyes and mocha skin. My heart went icy. In my head I heard Tamara: *Your parents didn't want you anymore. Their life is better without you.*

"Oh, please. I'm sure that's not true," Nora was saying to Jessie.

A soothing thought washed over me: We were all away from home for the first time. The stress was getting to everybody. Tamara was meaner than a one-eared alley cat, I was imagining things, and Jessie heard her dead brother. There were plenty of older kids at the school who must have gone through the same thing and come out the other end fairly normal. For us freshmen, the cracks were showing.

"It's going to be OK," I told Jessie. Her eyes were so glassy and dark that she seemed like a doll, but after a moment, she nodded. I sat next to her and gave her a side hug. She leaned against me, already seeming more like Jessie and less like a zombie princess. *And if you're not better tomorrow, I'll tell Miss Andersen myself*, I decided. *Even if we both get in trouble for sneaking out.*

CHAPTER 11

That night I dreamed I was swimming in an inky ocean under a sky full of stars. Flashing red and white lights reflected on the waves. Sirens droned in the distance, but I felt peaceful. *The perfect night for an end-of-summer pool party*, I thought.

Then I was back at the chapel with Rachel. Candlelight flickered through the stained glass and made Rachel look like she was on fire, her skin melting. She yelled, "Run!" and laughed at me as her hair began to smolder. She became a young man with emerald eyes and mocha skin. Jessie's brother grinned at me and rattled the chapel wall, the muscles in his forearms standing out with the effort. *Stop it!* I tried to say. Inside the chapel, someone screamed. I was screaming.

And then I was awake and falling out of bed. Landing

knocked the wind out of me. On the floor, wrapped up in my bedsheets like a freshly caught fish in a net, I tried to catch my breath. The sun shone through the crack of the curtains of our room, too bright. Confused, I glanced at Tamara's bed, but it was made and she was gone.

My whole leg was asleep. It was like having a rubber chicken for a limb. I gimped over to the desk and checked the clock. Seven forty-eight. My stomach sank. I must've forgotten to set the alarm. Class started in twelve minutes.

I'd already missed room inspection and breakfast sign-in. That was a guaranteed two points each — I'd be working four hours of work crew come Saturday, plus the embarrassment of being in trouble. On the plus side, if I didn't brush my teeth or comb my hair, I still had the slim hope of making it to first period before the tardy bell rang. I threw some clothes on and ran out the door.

During first period, I realized something was off. Even without the alarm, I never should have been able to sleep as late as I had. Miss Andersen should have woken me up at seven thirty when she came in to inspect our room. Five days a week since school had started, she gave our room the once-over before checking our names off on her clipboard. So Miss Andersen had missed inspection.

I didn't get to think about it too long, because Dr. Falzone, the dean of students, showed up at my classroom, interrupting our Spanish quiz. He raised an eyebrow at my rumpled jeans and bed head and pointed one finger at me. I followed him out to the hallway.

"You missed breakfast sign-in," he said, when we were alone.

I nodded. I was probably going to get some kind of dress-code violation points, too. My jeans had grass stains on the knees and my T-shirt was an accordion of wrinkles.

"What happened?" he asked.

"I woke up late."

Dr. Falzone frowned, like my story was a morsel of believability steak that he was rolling around in his mouth, chewing on, testing the flavor.

Someone's high heels *clickity-clack*ed down the terracotta hallway toward us, loud with echoes bouncing off the walls. It sounded like a one-pony stampede.

Miss Andersen stopped midclickity when she saw me and Dr. Falzone, as though she'd been looking for one of us, but now that we were both in sight, she didn't know what to do next. Dr. Falzone rolled up the attendance sheet and tapped it in his open palm, still frowning. Then he walked away from me.

"Do I have points?" I called after him.

"This is your get-out-of-jail-free card," he said, waving me back to class. He even smiled at me over his shoulder. It wasn't until later that I understood he was glad to have found me still safe on campus.

As I walked from Spanish to algebra, I heard a flurry of whispers in the hallways. You have only four minutes to get from one class to the next, and the language classrooms are pretty far from the math lab. So I didn't stop to listen. But it was like the Santa Anas had gotten into the people around me, with whirlwind bits of nonsensical conversation. Someone behind me whispered, "Suicide . . ." but moved away too quickly for me to catch the rest.

I guess part of me must have known something. Because after second period ended, and all the students walked to the chapel for announcements, dread started building up inside me. I wanted to drop my books and run the other way. Stupid. I filed into the chapel with everyone else.

Dr. Falzone paced at the front of the stage, tapping his sheaf of papers as people got to their seats. I smiled at Rachel. She gave me a wink.

Jessie's spot was still empty. Everyone else was pretty much seated. A few people were eyeballing the vacancy next to me.

I glanced over at Nora, who might know Jessie's whereabouts. She wasn't in the chapel, either. I got a bad feeling. No one missed announcements.

In desperation, I looked for Nora's occasional make-out buddy, Thatch. He was sitting center section, twelve rows up. He saw me and gave me a huge grin and a wave. I frowned at him. *My friend, who you've kissed in secret, is missing*, I wanted to yell. *Why are you smiling? Haven't you noticed something is wrong?*

Dr. Falzone read a couple of announcements off his papers — school play rehearsals, athletic schedule changes, work crew assignments, dinner menu. Floor announcements came next. A junior raised his hand: The AV club would project *Casablanca* out on the lawn in front of Hadley House Saturday night. Bring a blanket. Popcorn would be served. And then it was over.

All around me, students got up and left. Two girls

passed by and one murmured, "I heard they called an ambulance, but she was already cold." Dr. Falzone was still at the head of the chapel, talking to a junior named Jake. I made my way, against the current, toward them.

"Dr. Falzone," I said, when Jake walked off. "Jessie . . ." I was suddenly afraid to say anything. Like somehow, if I didn't bring attention to it, nothing bad would happen. But the look on his face when I said my friend's name let me know something had already happened. "Where's Jessie?" I asked.

He studied his papers for a minute, his brow furrowed. "Jessie Keita made the decision to withdraw from school. Perhaps you were aware she'd been dealing with a family tragedy?" I nodded, dumbstruck. Dr. Falzone smiled sadly and sighed. "Camden, I spoke to her at length. This decision was the right one for her."

I stood there, shocked mute. Dr. Falzone added in a kind voice, "Students come and go here more frequently than you might expect. Lethe is a wonderful, exciting place to be, but the pressure of the lessons here can be overwhelming." Then he scooped up his papers and left.

I went straight to Nora and Jessie's room. A crowd of girls clogged the hallway, clustered up in twos and threes.

Jessie and Nora's door was closed and no light came from the crack at the floor.

This was why Miss Andersen never came to do room inspection, I realized. She had bigger fish to fry this morning. *I wanted to tell Miss Andersen about Jessie.* Guilt stabbed me in the lungs. *Why didn't I?* The answer came back quick: *Because you were protecting your own hide.* I pushed my way through the gawkers and knocked on the door. No answer.

"She's gone," someone said.

"Get out of here!" I yelled. One kid bolted down the hallway. A sophomore girl turned her head away. The rest stayed where they were. It was like yelling at city pigeons.

I opened the door. "Nora?" I asked the empty room. Jessie's closet doors were open and I could see all her clothes and shoes still inside. On her desk lay her wallet, with her student ID under a plastic window in front. An ATM card, a five-dollar bill, two ones, and a twenty were tucked into the side pocket, along with a card for a free serving at FroYo2Go with eight of the twelve spaces punched.

I set the wallet back down and wiped my hands on my jeans, remembering what Jessie had said to me the night before. How flat she'd sounded. I'd told her it was going to be OK. This was definitely not OK. Who decided to leave school in the middle of the night? Without telling anybody? And leaving their wallet? Nobody, that's who.

The thing is that life doesn't stop. So I made myself stumble up the path to my third-period class, gut punched.

Tamara stood with a bunch of sophomore guys. A guy I was pretty sure was Shane yelled, "So is it true?" His friend elbowed him in the side. "Quit it!" A couple of other guys laughed and pointed at me.

I squinted. It was bright out on the lawn, compared to the dimness of Jessie's empty room. My fingertips were tingly and numb where I had touched her wallet. I guess I could have walked up to those sophomores so they didn't yell for everyone to hear, but they seemed like slow summer wasps. The angry buzz of their words lit up the part of my brain where survival instincts hung out. I didn't want to go near them.

Shane cupped his hands and yelled again. "I heard Jessie Keita killed herself because of you. *You* knew her brother was dead. *You* tricked her at a séance. And *you* did it on purpose." It echoed across the lawn.

It was like glass breaking, only it was the whole world.

Tamara's snickers broke the silence. She took a step closer to Shane. Her hip grazed his forearm. My guts took the express elevator to my shoes. I remembered Tamara crying that night she'd snuck out. I had told her what I had done in the chapel. And now she had told everyone. Worst of all, it was true.

I couldn't deny it, so I mainly concentrated on not fainting. I'd never live it down if that happened. *Get up to my brain and help me think, blood!* I thought. My blood was comfy staying down below my knees.

"I have to go to class," I said. It was the squeak of a mouse being strangled with twine.

"Killer!" one of the guys shouted at me, as I ran off. More laughter behind me. "Did you really do that? Hey, I'm asking you a question! Did you do it?"

My classes kept me straitjacketed into the day's schedule. Nora stayed missing and Jessie stayed gone, and still I was in class. Teachers called on me while I was trying to think. Had I scared Jessie so bad that she'd left school? Or was Dr. Falzone lying? Had she killed herself?

You can only freak out for so long before you burn through your supply of adrenaline and your brain gets dull and wrung out like an old sponge. When that happens, you can think again, if you are willing to go slowly. I went like a snail. Everything in my head was wreckage, and I wandered through it, trying to see if there was any small thing I could salvage. By the time my last class let out, I knew what I needed to do.

CHAPTER 12

I didn't watch Brynn's tennis match and I skipped lacrosse. I didn't look for Jessie or Nora. Instead, I went to the theater and stole Mr. Cooper's keys.

It was common knowledge that if you searched the theater, you could find three things that belonged to the drama teacher: the coffee cup he always misplaced, a pack of cigarettes he wasn't supposed to smoke on campus, and a warden's ring of keys that allowed Mr. Cooper access to the great unknown. Everybody knew about these items, because part of the Freshman Drama curriculum included Mr. Cooper stomping around, cursing under his breath, and asking if anyone had seen his stuff.

The key ring was on the makeup counter, next to a bunch of wigs.

What you are doing? I asked myself. Except I knew. I was stealing. In my head, that voice laughed from across the lawn: *Hey, I'm asking you a question! Did you do it?*

I stood there for a minute, thinking about Nora, and how I hadn't done the one thing she had asked me and how Jessie was most likely at home with her parents. But also probably laid out on a slab in the morgue. Either way, I had been part of it.

I grabbed Mr. Cooper's keys and put them in my pocket.

Cool as a cat burglar, I strolled out of the theater, across campus to the school's parking lot, where I hitched a ride down to town with Mrs. Sibley's secretary, Jude. I told her I was going to buy emergency Tampax at the grocery. Jude sang with the radio. I didn't know how she could be so happy when Jessie had possibly killed herself last night.

Downtown, Jude stopped at a red light and I got out. All the shop windows were decorated with orange, painted pumpkins and hand-drawn green vines. The streetlights were wrapped in black tinsel. It was only because Halloween was tomorrow, but it felt like I had been dropped off in an alternate universe.

The locksmith told me he would be happy to do the job. He said it with a sly smile and a thumb rubbed thoughtfully over the raised directive on each key: DO NOT COPY. While I waited, I went across the street to McDonald's. A bored, middle-aged manager stared somewhere past my head as I ordered a Happy Meal. I took a seat and looked at the tiny sack of fries and uncomplicated hamburger, but didn't touch them. I felt like Alice in Wonderland, and if I ate the food, I would shrink too small or grow too big. So instead I solved the puzzle on the side of the bag and waited to feel the right size again.

Half an hour later, I picked up my new keys, along with the old ones. Together they felt too heavy for what they were. Like there was magic inside them. Like they were the keys of good and evil. I put them in my backpack, glad not to touch them anymore, and started walking back to campus. It was a long walk, alongside endless rows of orange trees. But the road was straight, and all I had to do was put one foot in front of the other.

After a while, a car honked as it drove by, then slowed and pulled onto the shoulder of the road, kicking up a plume of dust. When I jogged up to the driver's side, Miss Andersen rolled down her window and said, "Want a ride?"

Her car was cool and quiet and smelled like coffee. It was nice to speed away from the scene of my crime.

"Quick trip into town, huh?" she asked, making conversation the same way she brushed the wrinkles out of her skirt before class started. On her dashboard, a bobble-headed skeleton in a tiny Hawaiian lei nodded at us.

"What happened to Jessie?" I asked, after we had been driving for a few minutes.

"What do you mean?" she asked, her knuckles blanching on the steering wheel. It was just one little thing, but it made me sure there was more to the story. I tried to rephrase, but I couldn't figure out how to make my question any clearer.

"Well, Jessie's gone," I said finally.

"Yes," Miss Andersen agreed.

"What happened?" I asked.

"Didn't Dr. Falzone tell you?"

"Yeah," I said. I slunk down in my seat and stared out the window. I could feel her considering me. I felt glad about the keys then. I didn't owe her to be honest if she didn't owe me.

"Well, that's what happened." She tapped the steering wheel with her thumb. The skeleton nodded in agreement.

At ten fifteen, after check-in, I went to Nora's room again. Now she and Brynn both had singles.

The light under Nora's door was on. Instead of going right in, I went back to my room to get the copied keys. I put them in my pocket and started back to Nora's. Was that a seam popping? Yeah, I could see how I was going to get kicked out of school: a pile of stolen keys squiggling down my pant leg, landing on my shoe like a big, felonious metal turd, and the sound of someone saying, "Hey, what are those?"

Then I was at Nora's door. There was no one milling about in the hallway this time. In fact, it seemed even more dark and deserted than usual. I knocked.

"Come in!" Nora yelled. As I walked over the threshold, I shut my eyes and pretended today hadn't happened. When I looked again, I would see Jessie at her desk and the weight in my pocket would pop like a soap bubble and disappear.

But Nora's room was empty. Not even Nora was there. She was sitting out on the patio. Already, Jessie's stuff had a dusty, pharaoh's tomb look to it. I hurried through the room and out to the patio.

"Where have you been?" I demanded. I expected Nora to be all zombified and spacey like Jessie, like she had caught some horrible brain-eating disease from her roommate. I guess I had forgotten this was übercompetent Nora.

"Crisis counseling." She jumped out of her seat and paced the patio, stalky as a wet cat.

Suddenly, I didn't care where she had been. It was Nora! I jumped right on her and bear-hugged her until she grunted. She tried to get away, finally gave up, and hugged me back.

"Ugh, get off of me." She laughed.

I pushed her to arm's length. "Are you OK? I was totally freaking when I couldn't find you."

She tugged her ear, looking superserious. "So . . . Do you have . . . ? You know, that thing I asked you for?"

It was like the keys became a live wire and shocked me right on the leg.

"Yeah," I said. Nora put her hand out and I gave her the keys. It was a relief to be rid of them. At the same time, it was as if I were sealing my fate. They sat in Nora's palm like a clutch of diamonds.

"What really happened to Jessie?" I asked. "Did she . . ."

Still studying the keys, Nora said in a loud voice, "I don't know. When I woke up, she was gone."

"What do you mean, 'When you woke up she was gone'? People were talking about an ambulance. They said she killed herself."

"Look, I don't know anything about that." Nora enunciated every word. It was like I was back in the car with Miss Andersen. I wanted to shake her or something. Jessie had been my friend, too.

"But what about all her stuff?" I demanded. "What about her wallet? Are you telling me she just got up in the middle of the night and walked out of your room and . . . disappeared?"

Nora shook her head furiously at me. I could tell she wanted me to stop talking. But why? Then her eyes got big and her mouth hung open in midshush.

"What?" I asked. She pointed behind me.

Brynn stood at the divider that separated her patio from Nora's. She was pressed right up against it, holding a piece of lined notebook paper up at eye level. Scrawled across the paper was this:

A man got Jessie.

Goose bumps broke out all over my arms. Brynn ripped the paper. Once. Twice. Into shreds. Then confetti.

She crammed the pieces into her pocket, turned around, and walked back into her room.

"What is going on?" I whispered.

"All I know," Nora said softly, "is Miss Andersen is going to clean out Jessie's stuff tomorrow. You know, to make sure it all gets back to her. At home. In Ohio." She handed me back the keys and frowned. "These aren't safe here."

The dorm door swung open. "Eleven o'clock! Get in bed!" Miss Andersen yelled down the hall. She came into Nora's room, clipboard in hand. "What are you two doing outside? It's lights-out."

I fumbled the keys as Nora passed them. They fell to the floor between us. Miss Andersen walked over and picked them up. I heard the dawn of understanding in her voice when she said, "What are you doing with these?"

But only in my mind. Because in reality, my hands were clasped behind me and the keys were stuffed down the back of my pants. Miss Andersen raised an eyebrow at me. "Well?" she asked. "What are you waiting for? Get to your room. Now."

I prayed the contraband wouldn't fall out my pant leg. Miss Andersen didn't even give me a second glance. A minute later, I walked into my own room and flipped on the lights.

"Ugh. Turn them off," Tamara muttered, from under her covers.

"In a minute," I said. She groaned. Too bad — I wasn't too interested in making her life easier at the moment. In fact, I had an urge to flick the lights on and off a couple of hundred times. But I didn't.

Someone had left a rubber skeleton doll on my desk. It was like any cheap decoration you could buy in the drugstore. Except the eyes were crossed out with big Xs and red marker dribbled out between its teeth. Underneath, someone had scrawled on a piece of paper:

EVERYONE KNOWS WHAT YOU DID.
YOU SUCK.

It was signed "Mr. and Mrs. Keita." Jessie's parents.

I didn't give Tamara the satisfaction. I tossed it all in the trash and climbed into bed. It was a weird world that the note from Tamara or her dumb boyfriend was not even the most disturbing message I had been sent this evening. In fact, in comparison to Brynn's, the bone man was pretty lame. It made me snicker to think that. Tamara huffed and rolled over, which only made me grin harder. It was an odd feeling.

I slept completely dressed, with those keys tucked in my pants. I was afraid to take them out with Tamara in the room.

Who was Brynn talking about? Why did she think a man got Jessie? Did she mean a man from an ambulance? Jessie's father? Dr. Falzone? I didn't know any more than I had yesterday.

I woke up in the middle of the night. You know how sometimes you sleep on an idea, and wake up with complete clarity? It was like that. In my mind's eye, Jessie walked off into the dark with a man. Not with her father, or an emergency medical tech in an ambulance. But a man with an old leather face. Barnaby Charon.

He stayed just offstage as I lay in bed, thinking how crazy I must be to believe it was him. When I drifted off to sleep, he danced out, full center, to show me again what I already knew. In some of these little one-act plays, he turned to smile as he walked away. Sometimes he was a horrible ghoul, a rotting corpse, a skeleton with Xs over his eyes. I screamed at Jessie to run away. Jessie smiled and left with him, anyway. One time, they held hands. One time, Barnaby Charon turned and pointed his finger at me.

CHAPTER 13

The next day was Halloween. When I got to breakfast, Mr. Graham had fake blood dripping down the side of his mouth. His face was chalky white, with big, gray circles under his eyes. He grinned at me with a mouthful of plastic fangs. His usual khaki-pants-white-shirt routine was disrupted with the addition of a black cape.

He sat at the sign-in table, eating breakfast with Mr. Cooper, the drama teacher. Mr. Cooper was four inches taller and balding, so I'm not sure how the two of them decided he would be the one dressed in a yellow-yarn wig and a flimsy red polka-dot dress. On Mr. Cooper's stubbly neck were two crudely drawn puncture wounds. They dribbled fake blood.

"Happy Halloween," I said.

"Boo!" Mr. Cooper replied, in a girly squeal, clutching

his hands to his sweetheart neckline. "You know, you get pinched if you're not dressed up by class time," he added, motioning to my jeans and white tank top.

"I believe you are thinking of Saint Patrick's Day and wearing green, Coop," Mr. Graham said.

"Oh, bite me." Mr. Cooper grandly gestured to his neck. They both laughed.

"You guys are dorks to the power of ten," I said, as I signed in. I would never have spoken to teachers back home this way, but there seemed to be a relaxed air between students and faculty here, since we all lived together, more or less.

"Muwha-ha-ha!" Mr. Graham laughed, nearly losing his plastic teeth. "See you in biology!"

"Costume room is open to the public! Grab a costume from the theater!" Mr. Cooper yelled helpfully, as I walked to the kitchen for grub.

Milk was contained in a stainless steel cow of a machine that dispensed moo juice from whole, 2 percent, and fat-free udders. I was milking my cereal bowl on 2 percent when Brynn sidled up next to me, wearing her tennis whites. Guess she had already been up and practicing. She leaned across to fill a glass with nonfat.

"Secret room. Four o'clock." Her breath tickled my ear.

"What?"

"Nora said to tell you. Four." She sipped her milk. *A man got Jessie*, I thought.

"Hey, I need to find pictures of people who work here at school," I said. I was pretty sure I could show Brynn the man who'd taken Jessie, but I needed photographic evidence.

"What is up with you and pictures?" Brynn tucked a stray hair behind her ear. "Did you try the wall of photos I showed you before?"

I shook my head. "I looked there this morning. Any place else?"

Brynn said, "Well, there's that room in the library. Archives, or something. You might check there. What are you looking for?"

"I'll tell you when we meet up," I said.

"Sure." Brynn nodded, casting a glance around the dining hall. Two junior boys sat at a far table. One winked at her. She sauntered over to their table without so much as a good-bye.

All that day, I raced against my wristwatch, trying to squeeze out five extra minutes to go up to the library and find Barnaby Charon's photo. I knew that as soon as she saw it, Brynn would identify him as the guy who took Jessie. But the whole world conspired against me with extra homework and teachers running over the bell and not a free minute the whole day.

When I was done with intramurals, it was 3:50 — ten minutes before meeting Brynn and Nora in the secret room. I played victory music in my head on the way to the library. I didn't know what we'd do when Brynn recognized Barnaby Charon, but at least I wouldn't have to be alone with my suspicions of the guy anymore.

The library was deserted. Most kids were still at sports, or getting ready for the Halloween party up in the dining hall. I jogged through the library to a room in the back of the building. A very small sign hanging above the door said ARCHIVES. It looked like a converted office. Cheap metal blinds were pulled down over all the windows, so I couldn't see anything that might be inside. I pushed the door. It was locked.

"May I help you?"

I knew the wavering voice belonged to Abby Claremont,

thousand-year-old librarian. She didn't work in the library so much as haunt it.

I was pretty much struck dumb when I turned. The librarian stood in front of me, holding a silver sword with golden flames curving up the sides. After nearly having a stroke, my mind registered what I was actually seeing — a kid's foil blade. The prop of a seven-year-old playing superhero. It was just that the light bounced off it funny and blinded me when I turned. Plus, old Abby was so frail and wan I could practically see though her. The gossamer wings and tinsel halo she was wearing made it worse. She was dressed as an angel. Because of Halloween, of course.

"Um . . ." I squinted at her. "I wanted to check out some old yearbooks and stuff. You know. For fun." Even I thought I sounded lame.

"Thou shalt not pass!" Her voice didn't wheeze above a whisper. She lifted the sword and bopped me on the head with it like she meant it as a joke. The effort practically toppled her.

"What do you mean?" I asked, ducking to get away from the sword.

"You need permission from a teacher to access

archives," Abby said in a normal voice, apparently disappointed that I didn't dig her fossilized angel humor. "We have books in there that are more than one hundred years old. It's restricted access unless you are doing some sort of school project."

"I just want to look for a few minutes. I won't mess anything up."

"Sorry," she said. Her face was lined, ancient. The lady had probably babysat Moses.

"Well . . . could you give me permission?"

She smiled, like her patience was at its end. "No, dear. It's my job to keep you out. It's someone else's job to try and get you in." She turned to leave. Her feet were in orthopedic Mary Janes. It seemed like she floated off on her makeshift wings. I kicked the doorjamb of the archives room. But softly, so she wouldn't hear. Then I jogged to the theater to meet Nora and Brynn.

They were arguing as I inchwormed my way through the tunnel to the secret room. They must have heard me, because they went quiet before I could make out what they were saying.

"Tell me everything," I demanded, as I tumbled onto the floor. Brynn held out her hand to help me up.

"That night after you told us about your stunt at the chapel," Nora said, unzipping her backpack, "Jessie cried herself to sleep. Tell you the truth? I was relieved. I got some sleep, too. But in the middle of the night, I woke up to Jessie talking with someone in our room. Except it was just Jessie there. She had that stupid broken Ouija board in her lap. I think she was trying to use it. Fine, whatever, at least she's talking, right? But then she freaked. I mean, gasping and crying and rocking."

Nora pulled out a tape measure and started constructing her precious door. Brynn aimed the flashlight so Nora could see while she worked. Unlike Nora, Brynn looked scared. Her eyes were wide, glassy beads. Nora went on.

"I said, 'What's wrong, Jessie?' She whispered, 'The seat belt,' over and over. I was lying in bed, trying to figure out what was going on. That's when Jessie sat up, quit bawling, and called out, 'I understand about the seat belt.'"

"'I understand'?" I said. Which was stupid, because I completely didn't.

"As soon as she said it, a car drove up to our patio, right across the lawn. The headlights lit our room up. Someone came to the door."

My skin went cold as graveyard dirt.

Nora grunted, twisting the screw into the wood. Her fingertips were white with pressure. "Three in the freaking morning, and I saw the shadow of a man through our curtains." She wiped her forehead with the back of her hand. "Jessie got up and went out. She didn't say good-bye or anything."

"Who was it — out there?" I asked.

Nora fished another screw out of her pocket and started working again, avoiding our eyes. Finally she looked at me. That's when I saw it in her face. Nora had been too afraid to watch what happened to Jessie — she probably hid under the covers or pretended to be asleep, so she'd never seen more than his shadow. *You're putting up a lock so you can hide from him*, I thought. It spooked me even worse that calm, self-confident Nora had been frightened.

"Shut up!" Nora answered, as if I'd said it out loud. "You weren't there."

"I saw him," Brynn said quietly. She took a deep breath. "I saw a man walk up to her patio and stand there. I thought he was her dad or someone to come pick her up — I knew she'd been having a hard time. Jessie opened the door and put something in his hand."

"What?" I asked.

Brynn shrugged. "Whatever it was, he was expecting it. It made me calmer, you know, like he was supposed to be there for sure. He took her hand and walked her to his car."

So that was the end of Jessie, I thought. The light went a little shaky in Brynn's hand. She said, "But the weirdest thing was? The man made Jessie get into the car's driver seat. She didn't want to, but he made her. He got in on the passenger side, then Jessie put her seat belt on, and that made her cry." *Of course*, I thought. Buckling her seat belt must've reminded Jessie of the day her brother died.

"What then?" My voice wouldn't go above a whisper.

Brynn shrugged. "She drove away."

There were lots of upsetting things about Brynn's story. Not the least of which was that when I'd looked through Jessie's wallet, she hadn't had a driver's license, only an ID card. Why would Barnaby Charon make her drive?

Instead I asked, "Why didn't you guys get Miss Andersen? Why didn't you get her when Jessie stopped talking?"

"I *did* tell Miss Andersen." Nora rubbed her fingertips together. She'd been twisting those screws in so hard she'd given herself blisters. "When she came to our room for ten o'clock check-in. She saw what Jessie looked like — it's not like I could hide it. I told her everything. When that man showed up later . . . I figured Miss Andersen had sent him. Or like Brynn said — it was her dad or something. Somebody who was supposed to be there."

I slumped down to the floor. "What does it mean?"

Brynn said in a quavering voice, "That man knew when Jessie was ready to go. The room's bugged."

"That's totally paranoid," Nora said. The skin around her eyes was blanched white, she looked so stressed.

"Tell her what happened to you after!" Brynn demanded. "Tell her what you told me!"

Nora went back to her work, despite the blisters. When she finally spoke, it was the quietest I had ever heard her. "After Jessie and the man were gone, I decided to get Miss Andersen. She sat me in her living room, made me tea, told me everything was OK, and went back to her bedroom to make a few phone calls.

"At around five in the morning, she took me up to the headmistress's office. Dr. Falzone and Mrs. Sibley were

135

waiting for us. They made me tell them everything that happened. When I was done, they told me to wait there, and they left.

"They left me there the whole day. Mrs. Sibley's secretary brought me breakfast. Then lunch. I asked her what was going on. She didn't tell me anything," Nora whispered.

I thought back over the day. By lunch, Dr. Falzone had already told me about Jessie going home to her parents.

Nora started up again. "Around two o'clock, Dr. Falzone, Mrs. Sibley, Miss Andersen, and two other men came in and I told my story again. When they left, I told Sibley's secretary I had to get out of there or I was going to go nuts. She went away and came back with a note. It said I had been in crisis counseling all day, and it was signed by the headmistress. She told me to show it to the teachers whose classes I'd missed."

Nora stepped back. The door was neatly secured to the tunnel's entrance. She sucked her thumb and looked at the huge blister there. Then she gave us a crooked smile. "What a joke, right? Not one teacher actually read it — they already knew the story."

Nora took out a padlock and three keys, making sure each key popped the lock open. Then she handed one of the keys to me and one to Brynn.

"What do you think was going on?" Brynn asked her.

Nora shrugged. "Maybe it's just like Dr. Falzone said." She ticked off each point on her fingers.

Index: "I told Miss Andersen that Jessie was having problems."

Middle: "Miss Andersen told the faculty."

Ring: "Jessie knew they were coming to get her at a certain time, and she got up to meet her dad or her sponsor or whoever."

Nora looked satisfied, with her three fingers out.

"But why get her in the middle of the night? And why the lie about crisis counseling?" Brynn asked. I wasn't worried about that. I was staring at Nora's fingers, particularly ringy there.

Nora smiled at her and shrugged. "C'mon. The most reasonable explanation is probably the right one. I mean, the other options don't make any sense."

I said, "Your logic has a big problem. If you were with Jessie all night, and she was spaced out so bad she was barely responding, when would Miss Andersen tell Jessie someone was coming for her? How would Jessie know to get up at a certain time and go with that man?"

Nora frowned. She started to speak and stopped.

I didn't know what she was thinking, but I was pretty sure of a couple of things: Dr. Falzone had lied about Jessie's departure, and it did sound like Nora's room was bugged. Also, Brynn looked like she might puke.

"You guys, what are we going to do?" Brynn asked.

I turned to her. "I know who you saw outside Jessie's room."

I told them about meeting Barnaby Charon on the plane and the girl I'd seen with him, and how it seemed like she was Drea Shapiro, Brynn's would-be roommate. Then I confessed how Jessie's elusive Mr. Skinny Butt might have been Barnaby Charon, lurking in the back of the chapel during announcements. But I couldn't bring myself to admit I'd . . . well, dreamed it was him. Instead, I finished with how I'd tried to get a picture of Barnaby Charon from the archives and had been denied.

"What does he look like?" Brynn asked. "How tall?"

I didn't know. I had only seen him sitting down at formal dinner and on the airplane. Also, he could have been old with a good plastic surgeon, or middle-aged with a lot of sun damage. I said, "Light hair, cut short. Maybe forty or fifty . . . or sixty." Brynn stared blankly at me. "He has luggage skin and cuff links," I said.

Brynn scrunched up her face and shrugged. "I'd know him if I saw him again, but I couldn't say about cuff links or . . . luggage skin."

"He was expensive looking," I tried again. My voice was too desperate and hurried. I could see Brynn's attention slip away.

"That's most men around campus." She rolled her eyes. I blushed.

"What were you doing up in the middle of the night, anyway?" I asked the question before I knew it was in my head.

"None of your business," Brynn said.

Except I already knew what she'd been doing. I jumped on the one thing I could nail down as fact. "You were sneaking out of your room! That's why you were up, how you saw onto their patio."

Nora's mouth fell open as she connected the dots, too. "You *were*! Who were you with, Brynn? That Troy guy?"

"Who says it has to be just one?" Brynn retorted, and I knew it was supposed to be a joke, but it came out sour. Her whole face went red. "Maybe it was Mark Elliott," she taunted me, eyes flashing.

"So many you forgot? Must've been a busy night," I snapped, flushing with anger.

"Shut your stupid, fat mouth!" Brynn shoved me hard. She had those tennis forearms, and when she slammed her hands into my chest, it knocked the wind out of me, sending me flying.

The first star in the sky, and the bubbles in the water. The hard scrape. I'm falling, I thought out of nowhere, as I landed on the wooden plank floor, thumping it like it was the world's biggest drum. I couldn't breathe any air in. *Now they'll laugh*, the rogue commentator whispered, in my head.

But the room was silent as a graveyard. I bared my teeth at Brynn, hating her as much as I'd hated Lia.

When I saw Brynn's eyes wide with tears, some of my anger melted away.

"They came after me," she whispered, holding her hands up. I had no idea what she meant, but all the tiny hairs all over my arms stood on end to hear her say it. She put one of those lifeless hands up to her lips, her face a mask of shock. And like a camera flash, for a split second, there was a ragged twist of duct tape across her mouth, gone before my brain understood what I'd seen.

Nora whispered, "Look, I think we can all agree that Brynn wasn't sneaking out, right? Let's . . . let's just agree to that." She cleared her throat, eyes glued to Brynn's hands. "Even if it was this guy — Barnaby Charon? — even if it was him with Jessie that night, he might still just be the guy who was supposed to pick her up. Right? He's part of the school system. Maybe it was his responsibility."

I thought what Nora said was ten pounds of cow flops in a five-pound bag. But I didn't feel like arguing the finer points right at that moment. I didn't want to be in that room with her, and especially not with Brynn.

"Whatever," I coughed as I dragged myself to the tunnel and left. With a lurch and a heave, I got out of there. Then I was stumbling back to my dorm, whispering to myself, "Don't think. Don't think." I filled my head with those two words until I was in my room, out of my clothes, and wrapped in a towel. I jogged down to the dorm showers: *Don't think. Don't think. Don't think. Don't.*

I cranked the valve to "H," waited to see steam, threw my towel on a hook, and stepped under the spray. The water hit my chest and my breath caught. Even though it was only a shower, something inside me shrieked with panic. I stopped chanting.

The silence was like the sound of a glacier cracking. My shoulders started shaking, all the way down my hands. I leaned against the tile wall and heaved out these silent, hunched-over sobs behind the flimsy pink shower curtain. A couple of people walked in and out of showers a few feet away. That's another thing you learn in boarding school: how to cry with all the loudness up on your face. Teeth bared, mouth hanging open, snot dripping everywhere, and every muscle in your face wrinkled up. Maybe biting the skin of your arm so your body could complete the circuit of understanding back to your brain. If you did it right, from the other side of that curtain, it sounded like someone taking a few deep breaths.

When I thought about arguing with my friends, and those sophomore guys yelling at me in front of everybody, and Jessie disappearing, I was in danger of curling up in bed and never getting out. That didn't even cover the freaktacular duct-tape hallucination, or how frightened Brynn had seemed.

Yanking on my favorite little black dress and glossing on my brightest red lipstick, I told myself I was absolutely going to go to the Halloween party. I needed to do anything but think about what had happened. Plus, I was much more likely to run into Mark Elliott at the party than in the girls' dorms. When I was ready to face the rest of the world, I swung by the props room in the theater and grabbed a glittery pink-and-silver harlequin mask.

As I walked up to the dining hall, I tortured myself with thoughts of what I'd do when I found Mark Elliott. Flirting at Lethe could be tricky. Romantic interludes were completely covert ops during the school year. If the faculty suspected anything, you and Romeo allegedly got your names on the List. That meant teachers kept tabs on your whereabouts, including "pop-ins," when faculty walked into your room without knocking first.

The trick was to find a guy who liked you and cram in as many make-out sessions as possible before the teachers caught on. Like what Nora and Thatch were doing — ignoring each other in public and meeting up secretly in dark corners of campus. Not that I knew any secret hand signals that might let Mr. Right know I was interested.

The dining hall had been transformed into a haunted house. A cold fog bank rolled over my feet, cottony cobwebs hung from the ceilings, and oversized spiders dangled above the deserted dance floor. The smell of dry ice was in the air. I spotted Nora, dressed as Darth Vader, eating a candied apple by the kitchen. Thatch also ate a candied apple, a few feet away. They were studiously ignoring each other.

In one corner, a carnival-style glass maze was set up. Behind its smoky mirrors, Rachel and two other girls bumped into one another, reversed, bumped into a glass panel, and laughed. In the reflected glass, I caught a glimpse of a pretty girl in a black dress, pink mask, and stylish bob. I smiled to make sure she was really me.

A tall figure in a yellow wig and a polka-dot dress circled the floor, sneaking up behind unsuspecting students and scaring them. Guess Mr. Cooper was in charge of tricks for the night. A few minutes later, Mr. Graham arrived, still in his Dracula cape, and took over the drama teacher's chaperoning duties. Mr. Cooper wandered off toward the faculty room.

I didn't see Mark Elliott anywhere. He was probably too cool to show up to things like school functions. I realized I probably also fell into the category of things Mark Elliott was too cool for. That was depressing.

Brynn was in the Rowntree Room, standing by a four-tiered punch bowl filled with DayGlo orange liquid. She was dressed as a cat. Or at least she was wearing cat ears and had painted black whiskers across her cheeks, but the centerpiece of her costume was a tight black leotard. A bunch of guys stood around her, and she was laughing like it was the best time ever. It was hard to believe she could be so giggly when I'd just seen her, a few hours ago, all tearful and scared.

I walked over to the punch-o-rama to get a drink. A tall junior guy wrapped a lanky arm around Brynn's shoulder. She didn't seem to notice. She laughed with some other guys, who circled around her. They watched her like those old cartoon wolf types, their eyes bugging out and tongues lolling. The beanpole hanging on Brynn was shirtless, with the word "!ooB" written on his chest in red lipstick.

It took a few seconds before I got it. Then I laughed. The letters were backward because he had written them while looking in the mirror.

"Boo?" I asked him. OoB Boy rolled his eyes. No goofy smile for me like he had for Brynn.

"It's supposed to be ironic," he said to no one in particular, kind of turning and dismissing me, like he couldn't be bothered to explain himself. He snickered to the guy next to him like, *Hey, check this out.* Then OoB Boy reached down and grabbed Brynn's butt.

Brynn didn't seem to mind. She made flirty eyes at a different boy standing in the circle. I was embarrassed for her.

"I dunno. You look like an Oob to me." I don't know why I said it.

A couple of the guys snickered. Oob Boy turned around. He was very tall. After a second or two of thinking, he said, "Oh, yeah? What are you trying to do, get me to kill myself?" It was even funnier to the guys around him.

"You're that girl?" one of them brayed. "Oh, burn!" and gave Oob Boy a high five.

"Hey, c'mon. Don't be jerks," Brynn murmured. She tugged at Oob Boy's forearm, which was now wrapped under her chin. Her defending me caught me like a fishhook in the heart, torn between being grateful and angry.

"Seriously," Oob Boy said in a loud voice, speaking to me, but looking all around the room. "You scared that girl into killing herself? What are you, psycho?"

I said, "You talk a lot of smack for a guy who can't even spell 'boo.' Sure you're not st-OOB-id?"

Oob Boy flung Brynn away in his rush to get in my face. If I got smacked, I would have to take my lumps. In a way, I was looking forward to it. My insides felt messed up. It seemed right that my outside matched. But before I even knew what had happened, Oob Boy got pinned against the far wall by Dracula.

"Don't. You. Touch. Her," Mr. Graham roared, his forearm under the kid's neck. All the fight went out of Oob Boy. The fight was not yet out of our teacher. You could smell something primal and electric coming off Mr. Graham. For a tiny second I was weirdly flattered he would come to my rescue like that. Then I noticed Mr. Graham's other hand pointed at Brynn, splayed on the ground. He wasn't talking about me at all. "What do you think you're doing, you grabby-handed punk?"

We all were a bunch of hoot owls, our eyes peeled open as wide as they could go. Teachers never touched kids like that. After a moment, Mr. Graham seemed to realize everyone was staring. He took a couple of breaths and stepped back.

"You," he growled at Oob Boy. "And you." He pointed at me. "Let's go." He stalked out the door. Oob Boy made a sarcastically gallant gesture toward me. *Ladies first*, it said. *Fine*. I flipped my hair out of my face, reckless with angry adrenaline. Marching right past Brynn, not even glancing her way, I led the Big Trouble Conga Line out the door.

We ended up in the faculty room. A fire burned in the fireplace. Mr. Cooper was snuggled up in an old wing chair, sipping from a coffee mug. He'd taken off the yarn wig, and sat like a man in his dress. His eyeglasses reflected flames. He raised a brow at us.

"Sit," Mr. Graham ordered us. He pointed to a scuffed leather couch. Oob Boy sat down, as far as he could possibly get from me. Mr. Graham stomped out of the room. Mr. Cooper went back to studying the fire.

After a moment, I felt pretty bad for losing my temper. I mean, sure the guy had been a jerk and poked me where I felt weak. But I had called him a name first. That hadn't been very nice.

"Sorry about the Oob thing," I said. He grunted.

"What's your name?" I asked him. I had heard it around. Trevor or Travis or something.

"What do you care?" he muttered.

"When I say I'm sorry, I mean it," I said. "Plus, I gotta call you something. Unless 'Oob Boy's' growing on you."

"I'm not stupid. I know how to write." His voice went up a pitch. It hit me all of the sudden: He was actually worried about it. Maybe I wasn't the only one who had gotten her weak spot smacked in front of everyone tonight.

"Travis?" I asked.

"Troy," he said into his chest.

"Troy. I feel bad."

He nodded. "Yeah, well, I'm leaving a note blaming you if I decide to kill myself tonight." Then he bit his lip. When he did that, he was almost cute. I decided not to say anything about his writing skills and whether or not anyone would be able to decipher it.

"Graham sure had his shorts in a twist," I whispered.

Troy smiled a little. I tried again.

"What do you think you're doing, you grabby-handed punk?" I whispered, all dopey. He giggled. So did I. From the corner of my eye, I glimpsed khaki pants headed our way and figured Mr. Graham was back.

Troy's trickle of sniggering stopped midsnuff. He stared at the man standing in front of us. It wasn't Mr. Graham. I closed my eyes, pretty sure I was going to pass out. Everything smelled like fresh soap.

"Leave us," Barnaby Charon said. Troy leapt like a small woodland creature from the couch, his footsteps light on the floor. My eyes were still closed. I couldn't get up the nerve to open them. Barnaby Charon sat next to me. Underneath the soap, I could smell all those secret smells that belonged to him.

When I did open my eyes, the first thing I saw was that Mr. Cooper had vanished. Only his steaming mug remained to prove he had been there at all. One of the big rules at boarding school was that at least one faculty member had to be in the faculty room at all times. Usually there were three or four. In case of emergency, you could always find someone here. I wondered if Barnaby Charon counted as faculty. I wondered if this counted as an emergency.

"Now I'm rather glad you didn't get off in Denver, Camden," he murmured. I couldn't look at him. My heart was falling down a staircase into some sort of panic-induced heart attack. It thumped in my chest with one big, painful thump and got back into rhythm again.

"It has been . . . amusing." He stopped, as if considering, then started again. "Yes. It has been *amusing* to watch you . . . develop during your time here."

The warmth of his breath made all the hairs on the back of my neck goose bump. It was crazy, but I wanted to jump up and . . . I dunno. Make him stop. Except I was already in trouble, and this guy owned the whole school. And there was no one to see what was happening. Still, the urge to unload a big dose of shriek 'n' slap on him was overwhelming.

"What happened to Mr. Graham?" I asked.

"He was not in the right mind-set to mete out punishment. Did you know," he added, after a pause, "years ago, Mr. Graham's own sister disappeared, never to be seen again. Now he attempts to save them all." He made a *tsk-tsk* sound.

Another missing girl. My legs got the shakes, like they wanted to take over and bolt on their own.

"You are afraid of me?" he asked, but not like he was surprised.

"Did you take Jessie?" I asked back. His breath stopped midexhale. It was almost as good as hitting him.

"And who would suggest something like that to you? What little bird?" Fingertips drummed his thigh. "Brynn Laurent, next door, perhaps?" He seemed like a slow shark in the water, circling me there on the couch, lazily debating the merits of attack over swimming silently away.

I didn't answer.

"I've brought you something." Barnaby Charon pulled up a brown gift bag by its handles and put it in my lap. There was something heavy inside.

He stood, finally putting space between us. I glared hot fury at the back of his knees. Like it was an afterthought, he dug around in his pocket as he turned to me.

"I have something for your nosy little friend as well. Pass this along to Brynn. She'll know what to do with it next time I find her." He opened his fist and dropped something small and gold into my lap. I thought it was one of his cuff links as it hit my thigh. It was so gross — like he had dropped a cockroach on me. I shoved the bag off my lap. It fell onto the floor with a *clunk*. I jumped up, finally ready to give him a hard crack to the face, no matter how much trouble it meant for me afterward.

Barnaby Charon was gone.

I stood there, gasping for air, trying not to breathe in any more of that soap smell he'd left behind. The gold thing he'd left me to give to Brynn turned out to be a coin. It was tiny — smaller than a dime, with no ridging on the sides or writing or anything. The picture on the front looked drawn by a kid and it was stamped into the metal unevenly. An eerie sense of familiarity overwhelmed me as I studied it. There'd been a gold coin on Jessie's desk. Next to her brother's photo, the last night I'd seen her at school.

I kicked the brown bag like a soccer ball. The paper split and gave birth all over the industrial carpet floor. It was Jessie's broken Ouija board.

CHAPTER 14

"So what do you think?" I asked Nora, after I'd finished telling her what had happened. We were sitting in the secret room the next day. The coin and the Ouija board lay between us.

"The guy sounds creepy to a factor of ten," Nora said.

"He practically admitted he took Jessie. He had to have been in your room, too, to get the Ouija out of her closet."

Nora frowned. "He still might have been acting with the school's permission."

"What about Brynn? He pretty much threatened to get her next," I said.

"That's not what he said," Nora countered. She picked the coin off the floor.

"You weren't there," I told her. "Plus, I'm pretty sure I saw a coin like this on Jessie's desk, the night she disappeared."

"Maybe it was Jessie's and he took it." Nora turned the coin carefully over in her palm. "My dad used to collect coins. I've seen a lot of them. This one is old."

"Can we look it up or something, find out more?"

"Sure," Nora said. "The school library might have a coin reference book. It doesn't look like a typical old European coin. If you're supposed to give it to Brynn, it might be some sort of message."

I took the strange coin from her. That fishhook in my chest still tugged whenever I thought about Brynn. She was selfish, but she'd defended me at the dance. She'd shoved me in the secret room, but mad as I was, I couldn't let twisted old Barnaby Charon use me to get to her. Simmering under those ideas was the sad feeling that maybe Brynn was trying to be a friend to me in her own warped way. I thought again of Lia. If my ex-bestie ever got in trouble, I'd want someone to protect her.

I closed my hand and said, "If Charon wanted Brynn to have this coin so bad, he could have given it to her himself. I'm not giving it to her until we know what it means."

"Comments?" Dr. Falzone asked, shuffling through his papers during announcements, a few days later. I realized

I'd been spacing out, staring at Jessie's empty spot, and looked away. Across the chapel, Shane raised his hand. Dr. Falzone tipped his coffee mug in the guy's direction. "Yes, Shane?"

"Um. Yeah. There's a new group on campus. Anyone interested in joining the Karma Collective, meet at the *chapel* today after lunch." He laughed once and shrugged. "Yeah, we're gonna *shake things* up around here."

People shifted in their seats. Dr. Falzone frowned, no longer perusing distractions on his paper, but watching Shane with measured concentration.

"Ooo . . . kay. Thanks, Shane," Dr. Falzone said. "Anyone else?"

Another hand went up. "Alan?" Dr. Falzone said.

A red-faced sophomore boy with brown hair stood. "Hey, Shane — Can you reschedule the Karma Collective? See, we're starting a group on campus, too. The No-Class Pranksters are meeting in the chapel today after lunch."

"Yeah, sure," Shane called, across the seats. "I wouldn't want to make your club disappear."

Scattered laughter echoed in the cavern of the chapel. A couple of kids twisted around, like they were trying to figure out what the joke was. Maybe twenty pairs of eyes landed on me. My stomach did a slow somersault. They were talking about *me*. About how I'd snuck out of my room after curfew and shook the chapel wall. I remembered the cheap rubber skeleton that had ended up in my dorm room. Apparently, the pack of sophomore bullies had me on their radar.

Dr. Falzone frowned, his internal Spidey sense, keen from decades of teaching, perhaps going off.

Shane half got up and corrected, "Karma Collective, meet up after —"

"OK, that's enough," Dr. Falzone interrupted. "I think we can stop here. All new groups must be approved by a faculty member."

"Sorry, Dr. Falzone," Shane said contritely. "It just . . . snuck out."

More laughter.

"Enough," Dr. Falzone repeated. "I want to see you and Alan down here after announcements." He didn't ask if there were any other comments before muttering, "Dismissed!" and making a shooing motion for us all to vacate.

I grabbed my stuff and headed out of the chapel, worried. I needed to get in trouble for sneaking out like I needed a hole in my head. As I made my way toward my next class, Shane called out my name, loud. He smiled like a shark, his group of buddies in tow.

"Hey, you should sign up for both those groups!" he called out, as he walked by. "I think you're a no-class prankster *and* you're going to get your karma." His friends cackled. The smile dropped off his face. "Everybody's going to know what you did," he said.

I guess that's another thing about boarding school: There are no secrets for long. And apparently, the subsection to this rule is that if someone finds out your secret, they can get a lot of enjoyment out of tormenting you until the story comes out.

For the first couple of days, it was taunts from Shane's pack of sophomores. I ducked away, ignoring them. Later that week, Troy became part of their group. He looked greenly unhappy to be there, but still he walked with them whenever they laughed at me. Whispers started up, same as when Jessie had first disappeared, except now they hushed as I walked by. I caught scraps of the rumors, though — I was a creeper, hated by my own roommate. I'd cruelly tormented fragile Jessie, chasing her across a dark campus and pretending to be her dead brother.

On Friday, I got out of the shower and my towel was gone. I stood next to the pink plastic shower curtain, dripping wet. And amazingly, for the first time in recorded history of dormitory bathrooms, no one came in or out as I pondered what to do. I was practically air dried by the time I understood what my choices were, took a deep breath, and darted down the hall naked, toward the relative safety of my room.

That one got to me, and I started getting angry. And scared of what they'd do next.

Nora stayed my friend, despite my new status. She'd sit with me at lunch when our schedules matched up. We met up to whisper about the strange coin and discuss Mark Elliott and Thatch. And when people said mean things about me under their breath, Nora would stare them down until they got uneasy and moved on. And they always did. Guess everybody knew that when a person like Nora chose to be friends with someone, it stuck.

In the meantime, I'd hidden the gold coin meant for Brynn in the toe of my favorite dress-up pumps, located in the back of my closet. Every few days, I took out the coin to look at it and wonder what it meant. It was odd, but holding the coin comforted me, like Barnaby Charon had put a spell on it, binding me to the thing. That was ridiculous, of course. It was only curiosity that kept drawing me back to it, and the idea that I was protecting Brynn was what felt comforting.

I also spent lots of my time in the library, trying to identify it. As it turned out, it wasn't easy to track down a coin if it didn't have any writing or dates on it.

A couple of times I considered trying to talk to Brynn. She wore Troy like a gangly, groping suit of armor. That kept not just me, but anyone with a gag reflex, a good ten feet away at all times. I figured it was better that way, at least until I knew what I was going to do.

The following Monday, when it was time for student announcements, Shane raised his hand and got up. Before he even started, my stomach dropped out the exit hatch.

He said, "Sign up to volunteer at our charitable faculty car wash Saturday. The Karma Collective will be washing teachers' cars and collecting a donation fund for the family of Jessie Keita. You can also donate old towels to help the cause!"

Tamara held up my towel, the one that had disappeared from the showers. She waved it above her head and shouted, "Hey, Shane, I have one for you!" She pranced down the chapel aisle. Of course Tamara was the one behind it. I wondered if she'd been hiding the towel somewhere in our room all along.

"All right." Dr. Falzone raised his voice. Tamara popped into her seat and grinned. Students whispered, not deterred by Dr. Falzone's frown or the hushes of advisors peppered through the chapel.

Dr. Falzone said, "Whatever this . . . *production* is about, it's gone far enough."

"But, Dr. Falzone!" Shane argued. "We've got permission and everything!"

"Yeah," Alan whined. "Mr. Weber signed off on our group."

All heads turned to Mr. Weber's seat. He was asleep. One of his advisees nudged him. He let out a big snore. I got the feeling it wasn't the first time he didn't know what was going on.

"Next person making reference to this topic can expect five hours of work crew." Dr. Falzone frowned at us like the entire student body was something smeared on the sole of his shoe. Tamara pouted. Alan and Shane smirked. Maybe three kids out there in the sea of my classmates looked like they still didn't understand what was going on.

That's when it hit me. Those bullies had me trapped because I was afraid people would find out what I'd done. But that was a trap I could let myself out of. I raised my hand.

"Anyone else?" Dr. Falzone asked. He did not see me.

"Me," I said, and gave a single wave.

"Yes?" He leaned against the stage and folded his arms across his chest. The auditorium went silent. Shane, Tamara, and Alan seemed very uncomfortable all of the sudden. In fact, Alan looked like he might puke. That was pretty satisfying, even though I felt like I might hurl, too. But mostly, I thought about this time when I was a little kid:

In fourth grade, a boy in my class brought a model dinosaur for show-and-tell. He and his dad made it, he told everyone. When I held it, I broke the tail.

"You owe me a new dinosaur!" the kid screamed. "They cost fifty dollars!"

Being supercool, like always, I cried all the way home. I owed fifty bucks I had no way of getting. And the worst was I *had* broken the kid's toy. Just like he said.

It took my mom until dinner to pry the story out of me. When I finally told her, she didn't scream at me. Or cry. Or wring her hands. Or any of the things I'd seen her do in my head. Instead, she put two twenties and a ten-dollar bill into my hand. It was the most money I had ever seen at one time.

"But it's just a stupid tail," I sobbed. "Some glue would fix it."

"Honey," she said. "You broke something that belonged to someone else."

I took the money to school the next day, sure the kid would tell me the dinosaur really cost a hundred dollars.

"What's this?" he asked me, when I shoved the sweaty, crinkled ball of money at him.

"For the dinosaur." I held it out, mostly trying not to cringe and bawl at the same time.

He shrugged and smiled at me, practically unrecognizable from the angry, red, screaming thing he'd been the day before. "It's OK. My dad fixed it. You know. With glue."

And like that, I was free.

That's what I was thinking while Dr. Falzone crossed his arms and Alan looked like he was going to pee himself. I said it all in one breath.

"I snuck out of my room and scared Jessie Keita in the chapel a few nights before she left school. I was playing a prank. Jessie was my friend and I didn't mean to hurt her."

I could actually hear the delicate plopping noises of mouths falling open.

"Someone came and got Jessie the night she disappeared," I continued, my heart racing. "I think something bad happened to her."

The auditorium roared. Most of it was a tidal wave of "She didn't just . . ." and "Did you hear that?" swelling around me. Then "*Got* her?" started like a riptide.

In the sea of shocked faces, one pair of eyes met mine. Mark Elliott's. While everyone else was freaking, he sat, perfectly calm. The corner of his mouth turned up in a slow, amazed smile. And I couldn't be sure, but I thought he said, *Wow,* as he raised an eyebrow at me. The word was an arrow, piercing my chest, pinning me to my seat.

"Dismissed!" Dr. Falzone yelled over the noise. Everyone stood at once, and Mark Elliott disappeared in the crowd. Dr. Falzone's finger hung in midair, pointing at me. "You. Stay."

In two breaths, the entire auditorium was empty. Dr. Falzone walked slowly up the aisle, hands in the pockets of his pressed khakis.

"Sounds like we have some talking to do in my office," he said.

The "we" who had "some talking to do" turned out to be something of a faculty party. Dr. Falzone called in the headmistress, Miss Andersen, and Mrs. Sibley's secretary, Jude, who took notes like a court reporter. We all sat in the headmistress's office. They drank coffee. I sat in a chair with no arms.

"Well, Camden. Let's begin," Dr. Falzone said.

I told them half the story, as if what happened involved only Jessie sneaking out with the Ouija board and me feeling left out enough to sneak after her. I didn't name a single other person. Each of the adults scowled at me, sighed, and asked questions. I probably should have been scared of getting expelled, but I wasn't. I guess it felt like free fall.

"If it was just you and Jessie who snuck out, how'd Alan and Shane find out?" Mrs. Sibley asked. The bell rang like it was punctuating her question. A moment later, I watched students flood out of their classrooms. In an alternate reality, I was going to lunch.

Miss Andersen gave me an encouraging smile. "Maybe you went with your roommate, Tamara, and she told Alan and Shane." She shrugged. "Is that how they knew? Or did all four of you sneak out together?"

Dr. Falzone tried, "You shouldn't have to take all the blame if you weren't the ringleader," and "Shane and Alan are already getting five points. They're going to assume you told us their part in it, anyway." He tapped a pencil on his notebook, drawing out the silence I was supposed to step into. "Maybe when you tell us what happened, we'll see they don't need the points."

They didn't know about the sweaty ball of money for the dinosaur, or how I didn't owe them anything. I looked out the window and waited for it to be over. It felt good not to tell.

In the end, they gave me eighteen hours of weekend work crew. Ten for sneaking out of my room. Five for commenting during announcements after Dr. Falzone had promised five points for anyone commenting. Three for being unhelpful during my own disciplinary meeting.

"You realize you are two points away from expulsion?" Dr. Falzone asked me, as we cleared the office. That was when the meeting was finally, finally over. I nodded.

"That means you can't be late to a single class. Don't forget," he said. And then something weird happened. He squeezed my shoulder. Like he cared about me. It almost made me cry out of nowhere. I glanced up to see if he meant it, but he was already walking away.

Later I found out Shane and Alan didn't get any points at all.

Saturday, I had to get up early for work crew. I dressed, then dashed alone through the cold morning air to breakfast. In the dining hall, I ran into Mark Elliott, who was eating early because lacrosse had a morning game. As I poured milk for my cereal, he wandered over to me.

"I was thinking," he said, as he grabbed himself a glass. "You want to go off campus with me today?"

It caught me so off guard, the next thing I knew, my cereal bowl pulled a total Noah's ark, overflowing everywhere. "I can't," I said, sopping up milk. "Work crew."

"Oh," he said, a small smile curling up his lip. "That's right. How about next weekend?"

I laughed. "Work crew," I told him again.

"Right. How long are you grounded?"

"Until forever." It was basically the truth.

"Was it worth it?" He leaned against the metal rail, studying me like he was sincerely curious. I felt myself blush, but not because of Mark Elliott's eyes on me. It came from inside, thinking how that pack of mean sophomores had slunk off, toothless and unable to get under my skin since I'd made my announcement.

"Definitely." I grinned.

For three weeks of Saturdays and Sundays, I worked from eight in the morning to lunchtime. I pulled weeds. I scrubbed chemistry sets. I hauled bricks in a wheelbarrow. Once, when they ran out of things for me to do, I had to dig a ditch and then fill it up again. I got sunburned and I was sore. My permission to leave campus was revoked. Every work crew session, a couple of new kids showed up for an hour or two on account of being late to class. I saw them come and go. I was a longtimer.

While I was helping lay a brick pathway one Saturday, a shadow fell over me. I looked up, expecting to see Mr. Abendando, the head groundskeeper. It was Mark Elliott. The guy seemed very serious standing there, watching me. Seriously good-looking, too.

I waited for that familiar, brain-scrambling, idiocy-inducing surge of adrenaline. It came, but only a little jolt. It was too hot out here, and I was too sore, and too blown out from all the other drama.

"Hi," I said.

"Hi. Will you go with me to the winter formal?" he asked.

It was lucky he asked me straight up like that. I guess if I'd seen it coming, I would have had a chance to panic.

I said, "Sure. If I'm allowed to go . . ."

"Great." He smiled, still standing there, hands in his pockets. I stood up and pushed my hair out of my eyes. I was wearing these big gardener gloves, and my face was sweaty and squinty.

I said, "You're not asking me because I'm a total pariah you feel sorry for or anything. Are you?"

Mark Elliott shook his head. I felt various parts of my body, not limited to my knees, go weak. "I'm asking because I like you," he said.

Here's the problem with hormones. Every night as I lay in the dark trying to sleep, it was hard to think about anything besides Mark Elliott. I mean, homework, my possible expulsion — they all slowly worked their way around to Mark Elliott. Barnaby Charon, Jessie, and the coin seemed like a bad dream. I'd be worried, but then everything would get fuzzy. And then it would get kissy.

I'd squint at the alarm clock, and it'd be two forty-five in the morning. *Stop thinking about Mark Elliott and get some freaking sleep*, I'd tell myself. After all, tomorrow was another day. And I had to be on good behavior forever so I could stay at the same school as him.

CHAPTER 15

"Come with me." Nora was in my room before I was sure she had knocked.

"Let's stay here," I countered. It was four thirty in the afternoon — that magical free time between the end of sports and the start of dinner. We could go anywhere on campus. But the thing was, daylight savings had ended, and it was almost sunset already. I was busy with homework. And fantasizing that Mark Elliott might stop by to say hello. You know, on a white steed with a couple of roses.

"Come with me," she said again. Nora was a big fan of repeated blunt-force verbal assaults for winning arguments. She grabbed my shoes out of the closet and tossed them in my lap. Luckily, they were my regular old sneakers and not those pumps with a gold coin sitting at the bottom of the left one. Even the thought of it getting lost made me break out in a shivery sweat.

"Don't throw stuff at me," I muttered. But the thing was, Nora didn't look good. Her face was pinched with worry, and she wrung one wrist with long, thin fingers, making a manacle for herself. Movement was usually Nora's friend, except when she got so tense like this. I put the shoes on and followed her out the door.

Nora led me toward the western end of campus. It was a popular place to go, because there were ocean views. The sight of all that water always made me gasp a little, out of reflex, like my body wanted me to hold my breath, even though the water was miles away.

The outlook was also conveniently located at the nexus of boys' dorms. My hopes perked up that I might see Mark Elliott. I was getting quite good at applying the chance to meet him to any scenario. Which was pretty sad when I calculated how often I actually saw the guy. Since asking me to the dance, he hadn't sought me out like I'd hoped. It wasn't like we were magically dating. I wondered if the dance itself would change all that.

Nora slowed way down, like she hadn't thought at all

about where we were headed. "I think I found out some-thing about your coin." She studied her feet as we walked.

I thought of Barnaby Charon plinking that gold out of his pocket and down on my leg. "It's not mine," I told her. But even as I shivered from the memory, I knew what I'd said wasn't exactly right. I wouldn't pass it on to Brynn until I understood what it meant. In that small way, the coin did belong to me. Or maybe I belonged to it.

"It's called a danake." Nora still didn't look up. "Per-sian. And old. Second-century old."

"What's that mean? Is it worth a lot of money?" I asked.

Nora shook her head and bit her lip. "If it's real? It wouldn't have a sale price. It'd be in a museum."

We turned the corner and headed toward a bench at the edge of the mesa. The sea was a perfect band of blue beyond the first twinkle of city lights. Two guys played Frisbee on the strip of grass next to the bench. Kids roamed to and from dinner and sports. Nora and I sat down.

"Why would he give a coin like that to Brynn? What if he gave Jessie one, too?" I asked, thinking about the gold coin on her desk. If only I'd looked at it more closely. Now, of course, it was gone.

Behind us, in the alcove of Hadley House, some girl

yelped, and a bunch of guys shouted. Nora said, "Here's the thing. Most danakes are made of silver."

The sun melted into the ocean as we sat there. The kids in Hadley House got louder. The girl shrieked one of those silly, wildly flirtatious, panicky laughs. I turned around to see who was acting so dumb.

It was Brynn, surrounded by a bunch of guys. They were joking around, halfway up the staircase to Hadley House, in front of that funny little Juliet balcony built to hold two. Shane and Alan were there. Troy "Oob Boy" Davis, too. Troy swung open the balcony doors and stepped out to look over the rail. Brynn followed him, beaming.

Troy grabbed Brynn and kissed her. He tickled her in the ribs. The other guys howled. Brynn pushed away and squealed, squirming back into the building, past the crowd of boys. It made me wary. *Get out of there*, I thought at her. Which was stupid, because out of where? The center of attention? Horsing around with her friends?

And then it happened. Those joking, howling, giggling boys up there moved like one person. They shoved Brynn back onto the balcony and forced the doors closed behind her. She stood alone. Then leaned over the balcony. It was too high to jump.

"Who will save me?" she called out, acting stupid. Too loud and laughing too much. Alan, Troy, and Shane bounded down the stairs and out to the lawn, leaving her trapped up there. The red light of the sunset reflected off the glass-paned doors behind her. Two or three other guys were still up there in the stairwell, holding the balcony doors shut so Brynn couldn't get back inside.

It was just one of those annoying teenage mating rituals. What did I care? I scoffed at the sunset. Nora was ignoring them, too, still obviously thinking about the danake.

So we missed the first egg. It sounded like a shotgun. I nearly gave myself whiplash, twisting back to see what had happened. Raw egg yolk slid down the window behind Brynn. Nora turned to see, too, her face paling.

"Hey, Brynn, I can see up your skirt!" Alan yelled, weighing an egg in one hand.

"Who hasn't?" Troy asked, his voice hoarse.

"Very funny, you guys." Brynn laughed, her Southern accent coming out. "Let me out."

Shane fast-pitched another egg up at Brynn. It exploded on the railing. Brynn flinched.

"OK," she said, laughing nervously. "You got me. Now let me down from here." I could see her considering her options. She put her hand up to shade her eyes from the setting sun. It caught her full in the face, making her skin golden. I'm not even sure she could see who was pelting the eggs. Brynn reached behind herself and jiggled the doorknob. Muffled laughter from the boys inside.

Troy threw the next egg. That one hit her high on the chest. Egg yolk splattered everywhere. I heard her gasp when it happened — it must have hurt. Guys gathered on the lawn, laughing and grabbing eggs.

"C'mon, Troy," Brynn pleaded. She was still trying to smile, to make it a joke. It looked like she said, *I need help*, but quiet, like she was talking to herself. I didn't know what to do. Steal the eggs? Go get help? Where were all the teachers? How could no teachers be around?

"Not so pretty now, are you?" Shane called out. An egg flew, smacking Brynn on the head, and yolk smeared in her hair.

"We have to help her," I hissed. I nudged Nora. Being confident, sassy, and powerful was Nora's territory. But my elbow didn't get a response, and when I glanced at her, her face was slack, eyes wide and glassy.

"The door's locked." Fine beads of sweat stood out on her sickly gray face. Seeing Nora like that was almost as frightening as what was happening to Brynn. Loud in my head, I heard that pounding sound, a fist on a door. *Let me in, Nora! Let me in!* Nora swallowed hard, choking back a sob, like she heard it, too. "No — it's *blocked*," she said. "There's nothing anyone can do. The door . . ."

Right then Brynn slammed against the balcony doors. They rattled but stayed closed. More laughter from inside. Brynn stepped back to the railing and threw her whole body against the doors again. I mean, she didn't hold anything back.

A moment later, she crumpled to the floor, holding her knee to her chest. The one she had told Mr. Graham always went out. The screams that came out of her were unreal. She curled herself over her leg. She screamed until she ran out of breath, and then she inhaled and screamed some more. An egg smacked the railing, exploding yolk.

The balcony doors flew open, cracking like thunder on their hinges. Mr. Graham stood there. His arms spread like wings to cover Brynn, who lay there sobbing at his feet.

Our teacher crouched down and picked her up. Their heads almost touching, he carried her down the stairs toward the infirmary.

"What just happened?" Nora asked, still looking dazed.

"Are you OK?" I asked her.

She gave me a shaky nod. Impulsively, I reached over and hugged her.

"Mr. Graham's got Brynn," I said. "He'll take care of her."

Nora sniffed and pulled away. Her face was already pinking up, the calm set of her eyes returning, even though there were a few tear tracks under them. "Holy wow — I don't know what got into me." She gave me an apologetic smile. "C'mon, let's go see if we can help Brynn."

I glanced back to see the pack of boys disappear in a near-silent whoosh of panic, probably fearing expulsion for their behavior. My blood boiled. But not for Alan and Shane. Those hyenas were beyond hope of being anything but mean. My rage was at the one of them who had cared about Brynn, but decided to go along with the show.

"You sure you're all right?" When Nora nodded, I said, "Good. I gotta go." Just then Troy resurfaced from wherever he had been hiding. He jogged toward the dining hall, putting distance between him and the scene of the crime. I ran after him.

"Wait!" Nora yelled after me.

"Hey!" I yelled, when I finally caught up with Troy. He wheeled around to face me. There were bruises on his forearms, and a cut of black blood pooled under the skin of his left eye. There was an egg clutched in his right fist. I didn't need anyone to tell me it was Shane and Alan who'd thumped him.

"Why'd they give you a black eye?" I demanded. But I knew. They'd had to beat Troy into going along with what they'd done to Brynn. He must have really liked her. I hated him even more.

"Get away from me," he snarled.

"You guys are monsters. What's wrong with you?"

He walked away from me. I grabbed his arm to make him stop. Troy swung around and cocked back his arm like he was going to hit me, or fire that last egg at me, close range. I was pretty sure he meant to do one of those things, but I stood my ground. I won't lie — I was shaking in my sneakers. But there was no way I would go back to ducking when a bully threatened me.

His face went red and his voice broke. "She was supposed to be *my* girlfriend. All this time, she's been going out with half of Hadley House." His voice spiraled up to squeaky and desperate.

"Brynn didn't deserve that," I said.

It was like I punched him. His angry face became unsure. His fist dropped. He studied the egg in his hand. *He's beat*, I thought, suddenly giddy inside even as I stone-faced him. *Now he'll slink off.*

But instead, he hung his head. "You're right. She didn't deserve it. Nobody deserves what we just did to her." He swallowed. "Is she OK?"

Never in a million years had I expected him to say that. "I don't know," I finally managed.

A tear streaked down his face. "Tell her I'm sorry," he demanded, staring at the egg in his hand. Suddenly, he threw it to the ground, where it smashed to bits in the green grass. I jumped back, startled.

"Tell her yourself," I said shakily. Troy squatted down over the egg and picked something out of the yolk. When he stood, something thin and shiny was pressed between his egg-slimed fingertips, and his face was slack with surprise. He turned to go. "What . . . ?" I started, but I didn't get to ask him anything more because he jogged off.

I was curled up on my bed later that evening, thinking about what Troy had said, when Nora flung open the door and strode in.

"We have things to discuss," she announced, completely ignoring Tamara, who sat at her desk doing homework.

I bolted out of bed. "How's Brynn?" I asked.

"I think she's in the infirmary," Nora answered.

"I'm studying, so shut up or get out," Tamara told us. Rolling our eyes, Nora and I headed for the patio. I was glad for the privacy, but it was cold and dark outside.

"Are you OK?" I asked her once we were alone.

"Fine." She waved a hand dismissively, as if she hadn't been shell-shocked earlier today. "Where'd you run off to?"

I told her about what had happened with Troy. Nora's eyes got rounder and rounder. "Well, good for him," she muttered. Then I told her about him picking something out of the yolk of the smashed egg. "Eww," Nora opined. "Like a chicken part?" I shrugged, not able to express how seeing it had tickled a weird part of my brain that didn't have words.

Nora surveyed me for a long moment and said, "Listen, you left before I could tell you the most important part of what I found out." She lowered her voice. "The gold coin Barnaby Charon gave you? The danake? Most are silver."

"So?" I asked.

"Archeologists find silver danakes everywhere. They weren't worth very much back when they were made — a bowl of barley. But the one you have is gold." She took a deep breath. "The only place excavations find gold danakes are in graveyards. They're coins for the dead."

I shuddered. "What do you mean? Are you saying he's going to kill her?" I whispered. "Do you . . . Do you think he's saying he killed Jessie? Or that Jessie's dead?"

"I'm saying that the coin sounds like a message, and it's not a good one."

A graveyard coin. I had told myself I wouldn't pass the coin along to Brynn until I understood what it meant. Now that I knew, I had to tell her. At best, she might know all about it herself. And at worst, at least she'd know some mummy-skinned faculty creep was sending her death coins.

"Check in!" Miss Andersen yelled, from inside the dormitory. For a split second, I considered telling Miss Andersen. But as the thought crossed my mind, I saw myself in her car, driving back to Lethe, how she'd stone-walled me. No, I decided. I couldn't trust her to help us.

Nora said good night to me and darted back to her room. I trudged in, shut the patio doors, crawled into bed, and pulled the covers up. I was freezing and scared, but I told myself to let it go and get to sleep.

Just as I was drifting off, I thought about how once when I was seven, I cut my hand pretty bad. My dad took me to the ER. There was a lot of blood and so the orderly put us in a cubical to wait. My dad and I waited for a long time, and nobody came. Meanwhile, my finger began to feel all cold and rubbery, and my dad paced around, muttering angrily about the no-show doctor. I got scared, and I started to bawl.

"Oh. Hey, don't cry," my dad said, which of course made me cry more. He glanced wildly around the room, like he was thinking about running away. Instead, he grabbed a box of latex gloves and blew one up like it was a balloon, pulled a pen from his shirt pocket, and started drawing. He made a whole flock of balloon chickens with finger combs and thumb beaks for me, and made them squawk and chase one another and squeak air, until the doctor came in and gave me ten stitches. I could still remember how Dad had held my other hand and whispered, "Squeeze as tight as you need to," when the doctor brought the needle over.

Thinking about my dad and those chickens, and how I'd held on tight, I drifted off, wishing I could call him, and knowing because of the time change, it was too late.

Brynn wasn't in any classes the next day. After dinner, I stopped by the infirmary. Brynn lay on a hospital bed with her knee in traction. She wiggled her toes at me. Her leg was like a broken kite in a tree, tangled up with tension strings everywhere, dangling from the ceiling. Despite the toe hello, her face was tearstained and she barely smiled.

"How are you doing?" I asked.

She shrugged and nodded to a chair next to her bed. I sat down. Neither of us said anything. Chatter floated in from the small TV in the nurse's office. There were two empty beds in the room, both with squared corners and clean white sheets. Dividing curtains hung from metal tubing on the ceiling. Everything was shades of sterile.

Brynn looked like a pressed flower inside somebody's old dictionary.

"Is your knee going to be OK?" I asked.

A tear rolled down her cheek. "Yeah." I wondered if she would still be a good tennis player or not.

"Those guys are worthless, Brynn," I said.

"What's my favorite color?" she asked out of nowhere, her voice angry.

"I dunno."

"Favorite food? The town I came from? What kind of grades do I get?" Each question was like the slash of a knife. For the first time, Brynn didn't look beautiful. A vein squiggling down the center of her forehead bulged out, and her lips were pulled back to show her teeth. In a way, it was the first time she seemed real, not like a girl who'd walked off a TV set. She must have seen that I saw, because she turned her face away from me. I prepared to evacuate the premises. That was standard procedure when someone startled me so bad I nearly wet myself.

"What do you know about me?" she asked the wall.

"You play tennis."

"Yeah. I'm the tennis champion. Since I was six, after my parents divorced, that's who I've been. Two hours of practice, six days a week. I played every country club circuit my mom could enter me in. You know why?"

I was afraid to move. I couldn't get over how she looked. Not pretty at all, and crazy for sure. But amazing in the way a volcano going off could be beautiful.

"So my mom could meet rich men. Some of those old guys liked me a lot. She didn't care. I was her ticket into that life. Without me, she was just a gold-digger divorcée who couldn't afford a membership." In my head, I saw that wall of trophies in Brynn's room, and I felt queasy. "Then I tore my ACL. Surgery and a year of rehab, but I couldn't qualify for a single country club open. I wasn't a ticket to anywhere after that. You said those guys I hang out with are worthless? I'm a tennis champ who can't play tennis. Tell me how I'm different from them."

She closed her eyes and lay peacefully, like a demon had escaped her. Another tear slid down the side of her face, into her hairline. Finally, I said, "Well, for one thing, you're not a total jerk."

"I snuck into Mark's room one night," she said. "After I knew you liked him."

"What?" I tried to breathe. "Why would you do that?"

"Because you liked him."

It was all I could do not to punch her right in her knee-cap. "You snake." It was what I'd wanted to say to Lia, after our fight at the pool party. *You snake. You pathetic excuse for a friend.*

She shrugged miserably. "I figured if Mark was the kind of guy who'd go for me after he invited you to the formal, you'd be better off without him. But he kicked me out. He likes you."

I wanted to yank her bald-headed. I wanted to giggle over the idea Mark Elliott had turned Brynn down *because he liked me.* Was she twisting her own selfishness into a story that made her look good, or watching out for me in her own warped way? Trying to process made my head spin.

"That's messed-up logic," I told her.

"Yeah, well. I'm messed up."

Brynn tucked her hand under her head. Her eyelids looked bruised. Under the fluorescent infirmary lights, I saw the crisscross of a hundred faded silver lines in the skin of her arm. After a moment, I understood what they were. Cuts.

"Are you gonna hate me forever?" she asked, in a sleepy-little-kid voice.

"Maybe," I said. But the thing was, I knew I wouldn't.

There was something about Brynn I liked, despite myself. So I said, "What's your favorite color?"

"Pink," she answered, half-asleep.

"Mine's gold," I whispered. "So we're friends now. That means you've got to treat me better next time."

I sat there for a while, wondering if she was going to be OK. Then I remembered why I was even there. I shook her shoulder. "Brynn," I said.

"Hmmm . . . ?"

"Brynn, wake up for a second," I said, and I gave her another shake. Her eyelids fluttered. "Do you know what a danake is?" I asked.

"No. What?"

I opened my mouth and then closed it again. I was afraid if I gave her the coin, she'd go looking for Barnaby Charon. Flirting with disaster seemed like it'd be right up her alley. I ran my fingers through my short, dark hair, nervous.

Finally, I said, "It's nothing," and started to get up, stopped, and said, "But here's the thing. You've got to stay away from Barnaby Charon. I don't want to freak you out, but he's a bad guy. He said . . ." Brynn's eyes were kind of vacant, like someone had already switched off the lights in her house and hadn't dropped the curtains yet. "He said he's looking for you," I finished.

"I don't know how I can avoid him if I don't even know who he is," she mumbled.

"He's the guy who took Jessie." After I said it, I considered whether I was telling the truth. I decided I was.

"What does he want with me?"

"He's bad news," I said.

"OK," she said. "OK," she knew what I meant? "OK," she would avoid him? "OK," she was going to go right out and hop in the guy's lap? Brynn turned her head away and snuggled up to her pillow. Her injured leg swung in its holster. That's when I realized if Barnaby Charon wanted to talk to her, she was a tractioned duck. Things hadn't turned out right at all.

CHAPTER 16

Later that night, my brain got busy unspooling all the stuff that had happened, and I had no choice but to lie there awake while it did. I added Brynn to the list of kids who were at school because something was wrong at home. Jessie, Brynn, Mark Elliott. Probably Tamara, too, since she knew so much about the topic. I tried to think about home. It was amazing how being away from a place could make all my memories seem like flipping through my great-aunt's photo album of people I barely recognized.

Like my mom. I couldn't remember how she smelled — only the way it felt to smell her. Or how hugging her made everything inside me slow down and get calm until I could hear the sound of her heart in my ear.

Or that day in my room, when I tried to tell her I was nervous to leave for boarding school, and how my mom had said, "You don't have to go if you really don't want to." But also how she had said it, sad and not meeting my eyes. A chilly claw wrapped around my heart and squeezed. My mom had been like one of those pictures where you could see two different things if you looked at it right — an old lady or a young lady, a cup or two faces — but you never saw both at the same time. One second I could only believe what my mom had said, and the next I could only believe how she acted.

It was still dark at 5:30 A.M., but I put on my clothes. Sneaking out the patio door, I got a whiff from Tamara's side of the room. It smelled like antiseptic and throat lozenges near her bed. Under that, it smelled like she had a night job as a grave digger. I didn't know what to think about that, so I grabbed my wallet and left. It was chilly outside, the sky purple with the not-quite sun. I could see the white puffs of my breath as I walked.

The squash courts were in the oldest and most dilapidated building on campus. As far as I knew, no one at school actually played squash anymore, and definitely not this early in the morning. But what the building did have was a pay phone just outside the locker room. And what it did *not* have, unlike by the phone in Kelser, were thirty freshman girls about to roll out of bed, pad to the showers, turn on their hair dryers, and knock on the booth door to ask if I thought I'd be off the phone soon. At the squash courts, there was privacy.

The square metal buttons were ice-cold as I dialed, and my fingers left foggy prints behind. I put the black plastic handset to my ear.

The phone rang for a long time. Six, seven, eight rings. I calculated the time change, wondering where my family could be and why the answering machine hadn't picked up.

"Hello?" My dad sounded like he had been asleep. I said hello.

"Camden?" he asked. Guilt knocked me back a little. It was like he barely recognized me. It hadn't been that long, had it?

"Hi, Dad. I thought I'd call and see how everything's going at home," I said, trying to sound like I called every week. You know — casual. My voice got all tight and choked up, though. There was silence on the other end, with only the sound of him breathing to let me know the connection was still good. "Dad? You OK?"

He cleared his throat. "Good, honey. Your mom . . . Well, she's sleeping right now. We both miss you like crazy."

I started crying a little when he said that. So much for my plans to be cool. "I miss you, too, Dad," I said. My dad made shushing noises on his end of the phone, like he was trying to comfort me. That made me bawl even harder.

"Dad?" I asked. "Daddy, do you think I could come home, maybe?" I didn't want to be in this crazy place with all these bad things happening. I wanted to be where people loved me and hugged me and took care of me.

My dad's breathing hitched and he sniffled. I had never heard or seen my dad cry before. Once when I was twelve, we had gotten into a fight. He'd been mad and walked out. Not just out of the room or anything. I mean, he walked out of the house and got in his car and drove off and left me there. He came back two hours later like nothing had happened. It had scared me pretty bad at the time. Hearing him actually crying on the phone was worse.

I realized time had passed, and he hadn't said I could come home.

"Just for a little while," I said. "Like maybe a week. A few days, even. It's just that things are sort of freaky here right now."

My dad groaned something under his breath. It sounded like maybe he was sobbing, except I couldn't fit that idea into anything I knew about who my father was. Maybe he was talking to himself, sorting out what to say.

"Dad?" I asked.

"This is hard for all of us, Camden. You know I love you with everything I've got. But this isn't where you belong anymore. I know that, honey. I know it has to be this way."

Disbelief so cold it became absolute belief crept up inside me and squeezed my heart until I thought I might die. My head got lighter and lighter, until it floated off my neck and up toward the roof. It got tethered by the phone cord I still held against my ear. Down where the rest of me was, I watched gray concrete under my feet warm to gold as the sun came up and gave me a shadow.

"Put Mom on the phone. I want to come home," I said.

"Leave your mother alone. Things have changed," he murmured. "Stay where you are."

"Put Mom on the phone!" I was standing in front of an empty building, yelling at an old pay phone. My father was gone.

I slammed the receiver into its cradle and waited for something to happen, but nothing did. I picked up the receiver

again and used it to beat the phone as hard as I could: *Whap!*
Whap! Whap!

Stupid thing was practically indestructible. I beat it
with no mercy. A couple of times my hand racked the
metal cradle. I couldn't stop, though. Blood welled up
under my skin and left hot blue bruises across the back
of my hand. I beat that phone until a tiny part inside me
stood back and said: *Whoa, you're scaring me.* Then I threw
the handset. It swung and dangled in midair like it had
hung itself. Like whatever part held my father inside it was
hanging there dead. It was true, then. My family didn't
want me anymore. The idea kicked me in the stomach so
hard I thought I might throw up. Instead, I fell against the
wall of the squash court and crumpled to the cold cement.

I didn't hear the bleat of the disconnected phone until
the sound stopped. Mark Elliott stood there, in his jogging
clothes, his hand on the hung-up handset.

"You planning to beat the phone to death, or just show
it who's boss?" he asked. It sounded like a serious question. I could hardly look at him. Everything inside me felt
wrong.

"No offense, but go away, OK?" I said. The idea of anybody seeing me, after what had happened, was kind of

unbearable. I squeezed my eyes shut and waited for him to leave. When I opened them, he held out his hand. I wanted to scream: *My own family doesn't want me, and I don't know why.* I put my hand in his. I couldn't help it.

We were too close when I stood up. He didn't say anything. He didn't step back, either. I could feel how warm his body was, even though he wasn't touching me. Maybe the jogging made him warmer than normal. Plus I was pretty cold. His breath tickled my collarbone.

I died a little, wondering what he'd heard. Could he guess the rest? Probably. Probably someone who was deaf with a vision problem could have figured out most of the end of that particular phone call, anyway. My chin started in on me, getting all trembly. The more I tried to make it stop, the more these sobs hitched in my chest, until I couldn't even breathe without them spilling out all over the place. It was worse than if he had seen me in granny panties, picking my nose under fluorescent lighting.

"Please go away." I tried to talk normally. You know, like I was the announcer on TV when the station goes wonky: *I'm having technical difficulties. Please stand by.* Instead, it sounded like I was being strangled.

He brushed hair out of my face. *This isn't where you*

belong anymore, my dad had said, and the wounds his words had left on me were so painful I wailed. Mark Elliott pulled me into his chest and gave me a hug.

Then I was crying. I mean, those ugly, hoarse brays where your mouth hangs open. I didn't know if I was going to die of embarrassment or shame or dehydration or what. He smoothed my hair down and rested his chin on the top of my head.

After a while, I took a few deep breaths and watched the rise and fall of his chest from the eye I had pressed up against his shirt. I swear, I could see the thrum of his heart beating. "Sorry," I said. He didn't say anything. I didn't want to look at the guy. *Ever*, if possible. But at the same time, I had to. Even if it turned out that he was disgusted with me. So I gave my nose a wipe and looked.

He had the weirdest expression on his face. It was nowhere close to smiling. Before I could figure out what it meant, Mark Elliott kissed me.

I'd like to say my first kiss was like being at the top of the Ferris wheel at sunset, and it tasted like cotton candy and jujubes. To be fair, it did start out that way, despite the fact that I could hardly breathe, and we bumped noses, and I kind of made a snorting sound once. But still — sweet.

Then there was all this other stuff. Like electricity. And tingles. And crazy-making, seriously impolite impulses. It was totally horrifying, but my knees actually did that romance-novel thing and buckled. He caught me as I slid down the wall and pressed me against it so there was no space between us.

Far, far away, a door slammed. Mark Elliott stepped back. The loss of every place he had been touching me was almost unbearable.

"People will be up soon," he said. My face got hot. We were no longer in the deserted otherworld of dawn. It was daylight — people were probably on their way to breakfast or their chores.

"Are you OK?" He used his thumb to brush a tear off my face.

"I just kissed Mark Elliott," I whispered. My whole body was still haywire. His kisses were made of awesome. Awesome, with awesome-flavored filling and iced awesome on top.

"What?" he asked.

"I like kissing you, Mark," I said, kind of horrified to realize I had blurted out the truth as my cover story. And I'd called him by his first name only. He wasn't some fantasy crush "MarkElliott" anymore. Now he was just Mark.

He stepped close again. "Yeah?"

Mark-Mark-Mark-Mark! my brain babbled, all giddy still.

I nodded and glanced down at our feet. They were in a four-shoe row, because we were taking up the same space on earth. He kissed my cheek.

"We're gonna get caught if we stay like this," he whispered in my ear. *Zomigod* — tingles. Everywhere.

He stepped away from me and bent down to tie his sneaker. Of course, he probably wanted to avoid being put on the List. And horror: I had called him Mark Elliott, like he was some sort of rock star. To his face.

"Yeah, better get out of here," I said, trying to sound casual, feeling the sting of tears in my nose. You know, general sob prep for when he left me there by the hateful, chipped pay phone. I straightened myself and tried to manage my hair back with my hands. He stood up. I waited for him to walk away. Except he didn't leave. Something stone-cold incredible happened. He held his hand out and smiled. "Let's get breakfast."

I took one look at the pay phone. I'd like to say I walked

off all happily ever after and none of the other stuff that happened before mattered. But the truth was, even when I took his hand and we started up to the dining hall together, I couldn't shake the feeling that part of me was broken, that I'd never go home again.

Gossip on campus wasn't like wildfire, despite the cliché. Nueva Vista County got a lot of actual wildfires, and so they were always showing them on TV. Those things burned and burned, and if you went to bed, you woke up to the news the next morning and thought, *Holy cow, a lot of stuff burned overnight*. Gossip on campus was not like that. It was like a weapon of mass information. The tidbits landed in the general pool of consciousness and you could almost hear the sonic *Fwoomph!* as they spread. They could get across campus faster than you could get across yourself.

Mark walked with me up to the dining hall and sat next to me for breakfast. He was the first person I'd seen flaunt the time-honored tradition of couples at Lethe pretending they didn't even know each other by light of day. When the weight of all the stares from our classmates got heavy, he reached over and squeezed my hand.

"You OK?" he asked.

"It's just . . . everyone's looking."

He raised an eyebrow. "You want me to pretend I'm not interested in you?"

Oh, man. I could barely breathe, my heart was going so fast. I shook my head no, my cheeks still raw from crying. He gave me a slow smile. "Good," he said.

CHAPTER 17

On the way back to my room after classes that afternoon, I passed by a guy talking on the pay phone outside Pilgrim Dorm. Seeing the phone made my hand hurt. Where was I going to go for the summer? Or winter break, for that matter? Not home, according to my father.

I decided maybe my dad was being held hostage when I called. That's why he'd said those things. Burglars had a knife to his throat, so he tried to get me off the phone. Except I couldn't make the idea work — wouldn't he have used his last words to tell me he wanted to see me again?

I thought about the way he had been talking, all tired and confused. Maybe he was having a stroke. No one had called to tell me because they were at the hospital, waiting to see if he pulled through. But the thought of my family circled around my dad in a hospital bed . . . and somehow forgetting to call and let me know? That idea was even more terrible than not being allowed to come home.

Finally, I thought about fourth grade, when my parents had been fighting so bad the word "separation" had floated around the house, from behind closed doors, and whispered through the phone line when my mother called her mother. That year, I'd practically lived at Lia's, our friendship cemented by the fact that she'd never once been annoyed when I'd knocked on her front door. Bit by bit, my parents had gotten better, and I had come home. Maybe this was the same sort of thing. Maybe in a few weeks, I could call my dad and he'd invite me home for winter break. The idea of staying on campus for the holidays, alone, made my insides feel scooped out.

When I got back to my room, Tamara was lying on her bed, reading a book. I sat at my desk and tried to distract myself by thinking about Mark. At first it was pretty good, with the kissing and stuff. But soon, all my worries got mashed together with those memories of making out with Mark, and so I gave up and took out my English homework. There was a paper on *Othello* due in a week. I was staring through the book when Nora showed up.

"I need your brain. I'm stuck." She crossed my room and opened the patio door. I followed her, glad to leave Tamara behind. Outside, she said, "I need to find out more stuff on coins. And some stuff on art history."

"Did you ask the librarian?" Suddenly, I didn't care as much about the coin. Just about Mark. And mainly about what my father had said to me.

Nora kicked a dandelion that had sprouted on the lawn. "I did. She says the books I want are in the archives. Which wasn't as helpful as it seems, because that room is locked tight. I need a note from a teacher to get the key."

"How about the key ring we copied?" I offered dully, wishing Nora could tell that I wasn't into this conversation.

She shook her head. "So far, those open everything in the theater, stuff in the faculty room . . . I'm pretty sure the drama teacher's spare car key got copied, too. But grand theft auto looks bad on your transcript."

I frowned at her. She paced, totally wrapped up in her own head. She was so self-absorbed. *My father told me I'm not wanted!* I wanted to scream in her face.

"Wow," I scoffed, instead.

She rolled her eyes at me. "I have classes, too, you

know. I can't spend all my free time sneaking around campus, searching for locks to try."

"Then don't. It's a stupid idea, anyway," I said.

That got her attention. "It's not stupid. Jessie was my roommate, and Brynn is our friend — that coin's for her," Nora said, standing up straight. "I'm going to find out what's going on."

I couldn't quite manage either a sarcastic comeback or a sincere apology, so I only shrugged unhappily. Nora flounced away, confident in her plan, as always. I stayed out on the grass, thinking.

"I'm sorry," I finally said, into the dark emptiness of the campus lawn. By that time, Nora was long gone. But she was right. Whatever reason any of us were here — I couldn't change that. But that coin did mean something, and we were supposed to figure out what.

A few days later, mostly to make peace with Nora, I snuck into the library and tried to break into the archives room. I'd seen it in a hundred old movies, so I was pretty confident I could do it. When I got there, I pinched my student

ID card between my thumb and finger and slid it between the door and the frame. I put my ear against the door and listened, because that's how people in movie land did it. Then I jiggled the handle and wiggled the card.

My failure at Breaking & Entering 101 was kind of epic. My card, with my smiling face right there on it, slipped through the crack and disappeared. For a few seconds, all I could do was stare. I had just unwittingly left a calling card for my attempted crime.

As I tried to talk myself out of fleeing the scene, I glanced around for options. There was an old computer terminal to the left, next to the water fountain. After a moment, my eyes focused on what was on it. A number-two pencil. I tiptoed over and grabbed it. I told myself to stop tiptoeing — I was in the library during library hours, not inside a bank vault. I couldn't stop, though. It was all the adrenaline, I guess.

I dropped down on my belly, pressed my face to the crack at the floor, and peered into the archives room. Right away, I saw my card, about four inches inside. My fingers couldn't reach it, but the pencil could. On the first couple of tries, I succeeded in leaving a bunch of graphite swishes across the magnetic strip on the back of the card. Then I wised up and turned the pencil around. The eraser stuck to the card enough to drag it.

When the corner of my ID appeared on the right side of the door, I pinched it and hopped up off the floor, wiping the pencil strokes off the back like mad and kind of giggling a little. I turned around to get out of there and bumped right into Ancient Abby. I won't lie — I shrieked.

"What are you doing down here?" she asked.

I knew I was busted. Even if I could explain why I'd been standing there shrieking, how was I going to explain the ID card in my hands? Full confession was a necessity. Giddy fear flooded my brain. I could see the future: I'd get suspended, maybe even expelled. They'd call my parents. Good-bye, Mark and Nora and everyone. I'd go home. . . . But wasn't that what I wanted?

My mouth unhinged and fell open, ready to barf out every little detail, when this *other* voice in my head spoke up. It was cool and calm, unlike the always-tell-the-truth voice that usually had the floor. It said, *Sheesh. Shut your big mouth, already. All you were doing was retrieving your own property.* After a second, I realized the voice was some strange combination of Lia and Brynn, with the self-confidence of Nora, too. But it was also me.

"I asked you a question, young lady. What are you doing here?"

"Leaving," the voice said with my mouth, and I walked away. The librarian made a well-I-never huff behind me. There was nothing she could do. Nothing at all. It was the best I had felt in a long time.

CHAPTER 18

Winter Formal was on Friday, and everything about everything made me want to pinch myself. That morning, Brynn got released from the infirmary, and school was over for the quarter. Break officially started after the dance, but even so, I'd already seen people trickling around campus with luggage bags. Their faces were full of nervous excitement to be free of Lethe, returning home or visiting old friends. Not me. Miss Andersen had signed a slip that gave me permission to stay in the dorms over the holiday.

That evening in Nora's room, Brynn, Nora, and I spent approximately a thousand hours getting dressed for the dance. Nora wore a black miniskirt that showed off her legs. Brynn's dress was bright pink and eye catching, but not slinky at all. I guessed she'd chosen it because it fit over the brace on her knee.

I checked myself in the mirror attached to the closet — fluffing my short hair, scanning my midnight-blue dress for loose threads, making sure my makeup was right. *This was Jessie's mirror*, I realized suddenly. After Miss Andersen packed up all of Jessie's stuff in boxes and took them away, Nora had done a good job of changing everything in the room around. She'd fashioned Jessie's old bed into a couch of sorts and hung posters of Olympic runners on the wall. But she'd left her mirror here.

"So, you going with anyone?" I asked Nora, raising an eyebrow on the last word to let her know I meant Thatch.

"Not officially," she answered, with a secret smile, blushing a little. "What about . . ." she started to ask Brynn, but then trailed off, awkward. Troy had asked Brynn to the dance. But that had been before the egging. When Brynn looked up at us, her eyes sparkled with tears.

"Hey, he's a jerk," I said. But Brynn shook her head and smiled the way people do when they want to let you know they're not really crying, but they're too choked up to actually say anything. Nora and I waited. When Brynn could talk again, she said, "Troy's gone. He withdrew from Lethe."

There was a moment of silence before I said, "When?" and Nora snorted, "Good."

Brynn sniffled. "He came by yesterday to say good-bye" — she raised a hand to stop us from interrupting — "and to tell me he'd just come from Dr. Falzone's office, where he'd confessed his part in what they did to me . . . on the balcony. He told me he'd handed Dr. Falzone a list of all the guys who were involved."

Brynn's hand was still up, but it didn't need to be, since I was totally speechless. "Then he told me he was sorry, and he left." Brynn took a deep breath, blotted delicately under her eyes so as not to mess her makeup, and gave us a watery smile. Down came the hand.

"Wow," I said. I didn't know what to think of Troy. Owning up didn't make him any kind of hero after what he'd done. But it did take him off my list of completely worthless individuals.

"So long story short, I'm dateless." Brynn gave us a grin and heaved a dramatic sigh into her pink makeup puff. A cloud of powder blew back in her face, ruining her moment and making her cough. Nora started laughing.

The puff flew through the air, but Nora dodged it with her usual grace.

Just then Miss Andersen rapped on the door and flung it wide. Her eyes settled on me. "There you are. Good," she said, and left.

"What was that?" I squawked, still flustered by Brynn's story.

"That is what happens when you get on the List," Nora answered. "Now they're gonna keep tabs on your whereabouts to make sure you and Mark behave."

Brynn turned to her mirror and curled the lashes of her left eye over a mascara wand. Her eyelid pulled way up, like she was on someone's torture rack. With her mouth yanked down in a small O, she teased, "Camden would have been smarter to keep it under wraps. Now she'll never have any fun."

Nora nodded in agreement, the mood of the room lightening. Like the two of them were sage poets hired by a Chinese fortune cookie factory: *He who eats cookie in bed wakes up feeling crumby.* Also: *She who sees boy in public will never see him alone.* I rolled my eyes at them, but secretly I was impressed with Brynn's ability to pick herself up from what had happened and go on. Also, my insides were bubbling with nervous excitement about the dance.

There was a knock at the patio door. Mark stood there in a crisp white shirt and pressed navy pants.

"Hi," he said. "You look pretty."

He looked only at me. It was like Brynn and Nora weren't even there, like I was the only girl in the world. In that moment I was so happy I might have died. Except I was pretty sure heaven's soundtrack didn't involve the smothered giggling of my two friends in the background.

"You ready?" He held out his hand. Blushing hot as a light bulb, I took it.

"Take care of our girl!" Nora yelled, as we left.

Everybody talked like going to Winter Formal with a guy was supposed to be a big deal. But it wasn't really. I mean, no cars or wild limo drives or whatever normal schools do. Just walking across the darkened campus, past deserted classrooms, up to the dining hall. Still, my heart was a hummingbird.

Mark and I didn't say a word the whole four-minute trip. Everyone we passed turned to stare, and I was stealing glances at everyone, checking out their formal clothes and fancy hair. I couldn't tell if Mark was nervous, or if my own nervous vibes were bouncing off him and coming back on me. I also couldn't remember if I'd put on deodorant.

When we got to the dance, Mark took me over to hang out with his senior friends. I stood there and smiled while they talked. Bit by bit, I relaxed. Little by little, I realized that behind the fancy clothes, they were the same people I knew. Mark's friend Beau remembered my name and told me I looked nice. I beamed smiles at him, grateful he was nice to me and to Mark, considering he had liked me first. Two guys — seniors, of all people — liking me? I would have never thought it possible. I wished I could tell Lia, if I'd been speaking to her.

"So . . . spring fling vay-cay," Beau said, and slapped Mark on the shoulder. "You going?"

Mark shrugged. "I'm going to see my parents," he said.

"You can't be serious," Beau scoffed. "I heard a rich alum is donating his yacht this year. They're going to Catalina Island. Sounds cool, right?"

"What?" I asked, as elegant as a princess, if that princess were also an uninformed freshman goober in way too much satin.

Beau leaned in close to me and said, with a knowing smirk, "The faculty host a trip over spring break. Last year it was a road trip down to Mexico. Those of us who've cut the apron strings are looking for a little more adventure." Beau threw a teasing elbow into my date's ribs.

"Funny, I don't remember you making any of the trips before." Mark smirked back, like it was an inside joke.

"This year, man. This is my year," Beau promised. Mark snorted a laugh. Beau started talking about lacrosse. I spaced. The disco ball did its disco thing, snowing bits of light down on us. I glanced out at the alleged dance floor. It was deserted. The music hadn't started yet.

Across the room, Mr. Graham and Mr. Cooper stood in their suits. Near them, Thatch helped himself to a glass of punch. He craned his neck this way and that, tiptoeing up on his loafers. He looked kind of like a prairie dog up on its hind legs, scanning the perimeter. His forehead smoothed and he dropped back down on his heels. I followed his glance across the room. Brynn and Nora walked through the doors, talking to each other. Thatch wandered over to inspect the audio equipment by the dance area. He smiled to himself, a little secret smile. *He likes Nora!* I thought. *As more than just a make-out buddy.* It made me like the guy in spite of his exceedingly high dork quotient. At least he had good taste in girls.

I excused myself to say hello to Brynn and Nora. Like an actual grown-up and everything. I whispered in Nora's ear what I had seen Thatch do. She said, "Oh my God, shut up!" about a million times before I was halfway through my story. Nora and Brynn and I became a giggling pile of girls. It was pretty uncool, but I was too happy to care. The music came on way too loud.

"Let's dance!" Nora yelled. The dance floor was still completely empty. I mean, it was pristine, it was so deserted.

"No way." I shook my head, still laughing. Nora grabbed me and Brynn and dragged us. "Brynn's knee — she's not supposed to . . ."

"You can stand there and shake your stuff," Nora said. Brynn grinned and nodded.

"But . . ."

I did not want to shake anything. Nora towed us out to the center of the dance floor and started doing the twist, with her arms and hair flying around. All I could do was bust out laughing. A couple of guys hooted at her. Personally, I would have died, but the commentary only seemed to encourage Nora. Brynn put her hands up over her head and joined in a little. A couple of other kids actually got on the dance floor. Then a couple more. Nora started a conga line. A stupid, time-warp conga line. And people joined in. I could not believe it. She had some kind of goofy magic.

"Oh, it's a party now!" Nora shouted. A bunch of whoops from the conga line agreed.

I had to dance a little despite myself. A guy from my Spanish class, Andy West, danced with me for a few minutes. And the craziest thing happened: I felt really, really good. Andy crossed his eyes at me and whirled around.

Then Thatch went right up to Nora and started dancing with her. At first she turned away from him, probably on account of their secrecy pact. He put his hand on her shoulder. Over the music I couldn't hear, but I saw his lips move. *Dance with me.* Nora's mouth opened in surprise, and for a moment I was afraid she'd reject the guy. But then she nodded, blushing like wildfire, and they started dancing. In front of everyone, for the whole school to see. I wanted to run over and hug Nora, she looked so confused and happy and embarrassed, and Thatch looked so proud of himself, the goober. But I knew this was their moment. I felt a pang of missing Mark. Where was he?

I stepped outside, looking for him. It was wonderfully crisp, dark, and quiet, with the party seeping out the door as it closed behind me. To the west, the dark chapel stood like the shadow of a sleeping giant. I leaned against the banister and wondered what Jessie was doing right then. The shadows behind me moved and I wheeled around. Mark stepped out of the darkness.

"I didn't see you there," I said. Because stating the obvious was one of my many charms. He stepped closer. "Did you see Nora and Thatch dancing? I'm so happy for them!" My cheeks still felt hot and flushed. I hoped I didn't look like a red-faced kid in gym class.

"I saw you." Mark half smiled. He looked very serious, actually. "Who were you dancing with?" Another step closer.

"Andy West. He's in Spanish with me. Did you see that guy jitterbug? I thought I was going to lose it. . . ."

He put his hands on my hips. *I no think good, Mark touch me when*, my head informed me. "You like him?" Mark asked, eyes focused right on mine, his voice a murmur.

I shook my head no. Andy was fine. Andy was even kind of cute. But he would never be Mark Elliott in a million years.

"Good." Then he kissed me. "I'll be in Nueva Vista over the break. My parents live there." His lips were barely inches from mine. "Could I come back up here and pick you up, take you somewhere?"

"Yeah."

"Call me," he said.

"More kisses, please," I answered.

"Ahem," Mr. Cooper said, from the doorway. "Why don't you two lovebirds join the rest of the festivities?"

"Hi, Mr. Cooper," I said, trying for a normal tone of voice.

"Camden." He nodded. Mark took my hand and tugged me back toward the party. Slow music blared inside.

"See you, Coop," Mark said, as we passed.

"Oh, I'll be keeping my eye out to make sure I do," Mr. Cooper assured us.

Mark and I danced. We had our picture taken together. We drank punch and hung out with Brynn and Nora. Then Mark went with the senior boys to get a group photo. By then Nora and Brynn were back out on the dance floor, but I was too hot to dance. I slipped outside again for some air.

The jasmine hedges near the doorway smelled a lot better than the dancing teenagers inside. I walked toward the breezeway outside Rowntree Room, away from the dining hall. Quiet voices bounced off the terra-cotta floors and echoed, overlapping. One of them sounded like Mr. Graham.

"Give me my coin," he said. The other laughed. I got chills so bad I thought I was going to pass out. I knew exactly what coin, and I knew that laugh, too.

Far, far away in the dining hall, the music went dub-step, like some huge heart having a cardiac event. Girls were giggling and catcalling. Mr. Graham's voice was like water lapping at a dock post underneath all those other sounds.

I peeked around the corner. Far down the pathway were the silhouettes of two adult men, walking together toward Hadley House. Between me and them, there was nothing but brick walkway, open lawn, and dim lamplight. There was no way to sneak up on anyone. I slipped out of my high heels and followed them.

Right away, the bricks made runners in my nylons that crept over my toes and unzipped their way over my calves. If anyone had seen me, it would've been hard to explain what I was doing, all faux-ninja style, trying to eavesdrop on a private conversation between the biology teacher and Barnaby Charon.

The worst was that I still couldn't hear what they were saying, only how they were saying it. It didn't exactly sound like an argument, but I could tell Mr. Graham wasn't enjoying his part of the conversation. I crept as close as I dared.

The two disappeared into the Hadley House alcove below Mr. Graham's apartment. I practically nested there in the jasmine hedge, trying to avoid detection, waiting for the sounds of their voices to diminish enough so that I could follow.

A door closed upstairs and the voices stopped. I snuck into the warm yellow light of the alcove and watched Barnaby Charon slink into the darkness near the sunset bench, like a vampire bat disappearing out an open window. After I was sure he'd gone, I crept up the stairway to Mr. Graham's apartment.

He must have been headed right back to the dance, because I barely touched my knuckles to his door when it swung open and Mr. Graham nearly ran over me. He looked a little crazy, actually. For one thing, his eyes were all wide and his face pale. For another, his hair was sticking up at the top, like maybe he had been tugging on it. It looked like the tail of an angry rooster.

"What are you doing here?" Mr. Graham asked. I noticed him noticing my destroyed stockings. Below us, footsteps and talk of ordering pizza bounced off the walls as boys came back from the dance. Mr. Graham started to step out and close his door behind him. I didn't have time to think it through — I ducked under his arm and darted into his apartment.

"Tell me what the danake is for," I said, as I passed under the bridge of his arm.

The sound of boys got louder as they came up the stairway. I waited to see what Mr. Graham would do. Finally, he stepped back into his apartment and closed the door.

He shook his head and the angry chicken tail danced madly. "How do you know about the coins?"

"I have one," I told him.

"You can't have one and be here," he said. His words were a dark chill slipping over me, sliding under my skin and sinking into my bones. I couldn't let him see I was scared, though, or he'd never tell me what I wanted to know.

"The coin's for Brynn," I said. "It's from Barnaby Charon."

His eyes darted all over my face. Whatever he saw must have convinced him I was telling the truth. "Don't you give her that coin," he said. "Don't even think about it anymore. And stay away from Barnaby Charon."

"Why? What's going on? What did you mean when you said I couldn't have one and be here?"

Instead of answering me, he paced to his makeshift bookshelves, picked up a framed photo, held it between his hands for a long moment, and set it down again.

"I don't know," he said, after a long while. *Liar*, I thought. The photo was of a teenage Mr. Graham, his arm slung around a tween girl with honey-colored hair. They had the same smile. His sister, I guessed. She looked a little like Brynn.

"She ran away," he said gruffly.

I said, "If you want me to keep the coin, then write Nora and me a permission slip to get into the archives."

Mr. Graham glared at me and I glared at him. The balance of power was way off between us. We were like two fat kids on a teeter-totter, waiting to see which of us would out-heavy the other.

"You need to leave now," he growled at me.

"I need that permission slip," I told him.

He turned on his heel and went into the kitchen. He slammed a couple of drawers in there. A moment later, he returned and thrust a piece of paper into my hand. Then I stumbled out the door.

Out on the thick grass near Hadley House, I unfolded the paper. On a piece of school letterhead, he had written:

Ms. Claremont:
Nora and Camden are working on an independent project. Please allow them access to the archival section in the library with my permission.
—Henry Graham

I ran back to the dance, barefoot and giddy. The lights blazed inside, but students were walking out, laughing, and horsing around, and I knew the dance must be over. Sure enough, the dining hall was nearly empty. Gold and silver balloons were strewn across the floor, the remnants of some grand finale. Nora and Thatch were the lone slow dancers on the dance floor. I hesitated, not wanting to interrupt them, but pretty sure Nora would want to see the note.

"Try not to think too harshly of him," Mr. Cooper said, practically right in my ear. I jumped about a foot, startled. He wore a navy blazer, khaki pants, and a sad smile.

"Who?" I asked, wondering if Mark had gotten into some sort of trouble while I'd been gone.

"All of them. But Henry Graham, for one. Teachers here are like students, except they've made more mistakes. The sooner you understand, the wiser you will be."

Mr. Cooper must've seen me sneak off after Mr. Graham — after all, I was on the List now. Still, what he'd said was odd. "I'm not sure I understand," I half apologized, giving him a wobbly smile. He was the drama teacher, I told myself. Melodramatic flair was part of his paycheck.

Mr. Cooper leaned closer, conspiring and lecturing in the same voice. "Surely you've heard the rumors?" I shook my head, hypnotized by the rasp of his voice, his calm brown eyes behind the wire-rimmed glasses. "They say Dr. Falzone used to be a drinker. One night he got behind the wheel and killed three teens who were driving home from a football game. He hasn't had a drink since, turned his life around, came here. He keeps a single bottle of unopened whisky in his desk. Just in case."

I scoffed, trying for a laugh. "You're teasing me. You made that up," I said. But for some reason, I thought of Mr. Graham holding his sister's picture.

Mr. Cooper smiled. "How about our dear Miss Andersen? You'd hardly believe she once poisoned her sister. An adolescent impulse. They were rivals for the same young man. 'Just a little,' Miss Andersen told the police. 'Just to make her sick for their date.' You'll notice how she's not allowed in the kitchen here."

There was something so honest in his face that I didn't know if I'd explode with laughter or believe him and maybe throw up.

"If that's true," I said slowly, "then tell me what Barnaby Charon did."

He raised an eyebrow at me. "He has no story, as he is neither teacher nor student." All the hairs on my arms stood up when he said that. Of course, that was the kind of reaction Mr. Cooper seemed to love drawing out of people.

"You're a teacher. Why are you here? What did you do?" I asked.

Mr. Cooper's hypnotic smile broke and he stepped back. Fresh air whooshed onto my face, and then he was simply a drama teacher in a worn navy blazer, trying to prank a freshman. I couldn't believe I'd almost fallen for it. He chuckled. "Why, only what happens to us all. I made a mistake."

I laughed, relieved to be past his spookiness. "You had me going there for a minute. Have you seen Mark?" I glanced at the dance floor, but now it was completely empty. No sign of Nora or Thatch anywhere. Shoot.

"I think that young man has gone home," Mr. Cooper said, a wistful tone in his voice. I furrowed my brow. He meant the dorms, right? I didn't ask, though. I'd had enough of Mr. Cooper and his pranks. Besides, it was almost ten. Time for check-in.

"Well, thanks," I said. "Gotta go." I hurried toward the breezeway, where I'd dropped my shoes. Furtively, I glanced around for any sight of Mark, feeling guilty I'd ditched him. I didn't see him anywhere.

"You kids have it so easy!" Mr. Cooper called. I ran all the way back to the dorms, the sound of his laughter trailing after me.

CHAPTER 19

I woke up around noon, and by then campus was pretty much deserted. Winter break had started. I raced right over to Nora's room to show her the note from Mr. Graham, but she'd already left. There was an empty, hollow feel to the dorm. With no snatches of conversations behind doorways or hair dryers going in the bathroom, the place felt like a dried-out piece of wood.

I threw on some clothes and ran up to the archives room, but the whole library was closed for the holiday. Disappointed, I stole over to Hadley House and checked out Mark's balcony window to see if he was still on campus. The doors were closed, the shades were drawn, and it was dark. He was gone without even a good-bye. A dull ache filled up my chest. I didn't know whether to be mad at him or myself. After all, I was the one who'd left the dance.

One rainy Saturday when I was a kid, I saw a movie on TV about an astronaut. He had to fix something on the outside of the spaceship, and so he got in his gear and went into the zero-gravity blackness of space. The whole time, you could see Earth behind him, so far away and tiny. Just watching, you knew the astronaut's flimsy tether was probably going to break and send him floating away from the spaceship, and away from Earth, and into the unknowable cold darkness, unconnected to anything and unable to ever return.

As I drifted across the deserted campus, I felt like that astronaut. I was thinking about Mark, and about Barnaby Charon, and what was in that archives room. But another part of me was trying not to panic over the feeling that I was too far away from home, and this empty school was my tiny spaceship, and the phone call to my dad had been my tether.

So later in the afternoon, I called home again. I let the phone ring until the rim of my ear hurt. No one answered. I called again that night. Then at one thirty in the morning, I snuck out of my room and called on the dorm phone. After that last time, I could almost feel my parents on the other side, watching the phone, not picking it up. I slept late the next day. The first thing I did when I rolled out of bed was to pad over to the dorm phone. I was on a mission to make my parents talk to me.

But the thing was, when I put my finger on the button, I couldn't move. I stood there, touching the button marked 1 for a while. Then I dialed Mark's number.

"I missed you," he said, when he heard my voice. My heart shivered in my chest.

"Come get me," I told him.

Two hours later, we were on a city bus going through Nueva Vista, sitting in blue plastic bus seats, thigh to thigh. He stretched his arm across the back of my seat and wrapped his hand around my shoulder. Once, he rested his chin on the top of my head and smelled my hair. Each time he did something like that, my astronaut stomach found gravity and I connected to the earth again. It was hard not to fall in love with him a little.

I glanced out the scratched Plexiglas window. We were in a residential neighborhood.

"Let's get off here," Mark said, as the brakes hissed and the bus lurched to a stop. I'd already guessed we were going to Salinas Street, to a movie, to the zoo, and out to lunch. I'd been shot down each time.

We got out and walked up a few side streets, getting peeks of the ocean over the rooftops and greenery. Nueva Vista was a little bit like heaven, if your idea of heaven involves a lot of people and beaches everywhere. I liked the smell. Everything was always in bloom, and you never saw it rain, but the grass was always kind of damp. Whenever the ocean came into view, though, I'd flinch a little.

"You don't like the water," Mark said.

"My friend Lia used to say she was afraid of heights. But when she talked about it, her real fear was she'd be somewhere up high and feel compelled to jump." I shrugged, watching the sunlight glint off distant waves. "I'm that way about water, like if I got close enough, I'd have an overwhelming urge to dive in headfirst. It freaks me out."

"Can you swim?" he asked.

"Yeah. It doesn't matter, though. Weird, huh?"

"Well, then, no beach dates. I promise." Mark grabbed my hand and walked up the front drive of a house.

"This is where my family lives."

The way he'd said it, so nervous and happy, my heart fluttered. I was glad he hadn't told me where we were going, so I didn't have too much time to freak out about meeting his family. Still, in the twenty seconds it took to make it to the door, granules of freaked-out-ness collected at the pit of my stomach, scratching my innards as they swirled around. We went inside.

My first thought was how everything in Mark's house looked welcoming. Like you could curl right up on the love seat and snuggle into the perfectly fluffed cushions. An ivory linen couch stood in front of the fireplace, a soft gold throw folded over one arm. A black-and-white cat peered at us from the windowsill.

Under that comfy feeling, something wasn't quite right. Like when you eat one of those fat-free, sugar-free candies, and at first your taste buds are all, "This is awesome!" but then the flavor changes somehow, and goes all fakey too sweet, and before you can even finish the thought, your mouth is already changing its mind. The house was like that.

Mark held my hand too tight — until the bones squeezed together. I didn't say anything. I wasn't sure Mark was breathing anymore. I thought about what Brynn had told me at the tennis courts: Mark was the kid who got sent to boarding school. His brother stayed at home.

He led me through the house, his hand cold and formal in mine. In the hallway upstairs, he opened the door to our right. Inside, there was a bed with a dark blue spread and a desk with a lamp on it.

"This is my room," he said. There were no pictures on the walls. No knickknacks. It even smelled empty. The sound of a ringing phone line buzzed through my head. Mark stepped back into the hall. Then he opened the door across the way and went in.

The second room had the same bedspread, but that was the only similarity. These walls were papered with photos — some framed, some tacked up. Most included the smiling face of Mark Elliott. There was a bookcase filled with sports trophies. Tennis and baseball. It was what I had imagined Mark's room would look like. For a second, I thought maybe he'd been deadpanning a joke I didn't get — he had shown me the guest room first. I took a step inside.

It wasn't Mark in the pictures. The hair was a little darker, the face fuller. I walked over to the trophy case. JOHN ELLIOTT glinted at me from a dozen tiny plaques. It was his brother's room. I stepped back and bumped into a laundry hamper. A Stonehenge of dirty white socks and discarded shorts lay in a semicircle on the floor in front of it.

"I want you to know about me," he said.

"Oh."

Mark dropped my hand. "Hi, Mom," he said.

She brushed right past us, holding a basket of folded laundry. I didn't know if we were in trouble or not, unsupervised and uninvited in her house. She crammed tighty-whiteys into a drawer rapid fire, like she was armed with a semiautomatic underwear stuffer.

Since she wasn't looking at us, I looked at her. Mark's mom seemed exactly like the house she lived in — like under the perfect makeup and sparkly bracelet and great tan, she was a woman who knew her husband's secretary got paid too much.

Mark's mom laughed under her breath, and for a panicky moment, I thought she'd read my mind. She closed the drawer and said, "You're always in your brother's room. Why is that, I wonder?"

Mark's whole face lit up, like he didn't notice how awful her body language was. Maybe he was used to it. "I brought home a friend, Mom." He stepped toward her. Mrs. Elliott's shoulders hunched up. She put her hands down flat on the top of the dresser and stared out the window, and she was angry. It must have been bad, because even Mark stopped trying to get closer to her.

"I will always love you, Marky. But you can't do this — come back here — anymore. It's too painful for me," she said.

"Too painful for *you*?" he yelled. I jumped and covered my ears. I swear, the windows rattled.

No one moved. I was pretty sure that if I could've gotten even one of my muscles in gear, I'd have taken off running. Mark's mom was intent on the window, her face hard. I wished she'd at least glance at him. No mom could stay mad when her own kid looked like Mark did right then.

"Mom?"

"Get out," she whispered. "Let me go. Let me get on with my life. Please, God, please."

I went back to campus that day, but Mark didn't. Three days later, he showed back up at school. I didn't ask where he'd been. Back home? To a hotel?

I'd been kind of relieved when he was gone, actually. It took three days to figure out what to say to him.

We found a shady part of lawn underneath an olive tree and kissed, slow and lazy. It was the middle of the day. About every half an hour or so, a groundskeeper swung by in his little golf cart, but we could hear him coming a mile away.

"Why did you want me to see your house?" I asked, after we'd been lying there for a while.

"To get sympathy," he whispered into my neck. "Don't you feel bad for me? My mom hates me. Kiss me and make it better." He leaned in.

I wasn't about to get sidetracked. I said, "I'm serious."

He bit his bottom lip, like he was thinking. "That day you stood up in announcements and told everyone you'd snuck out." He smiled at the memory, even as I squirmed. "If you could've seen yourself, you'd know how I feel." He paused, staring past me, distracted by his own thoughts. In that moment, I wondered if he loved me. The idea stunned me with happiness. "You're brave. I like that."

We lay there, forehead to forehead, breathing the same air.

"What happened with your family?" I asked him.

"I don't know," Mark said.

I got chills, thinking about the phone call to my father.

How right before I'd called, I had known *and* hadn't known what would happen, all at the same time. Mark looked like that, like the knowing and the not knowing were battling it out somewhere dark in his head. I snuggled up and he kissed my neck and I tried to concentrate on what it felt like to lie in the grass with Mark Elliott. Because: awesome.

Except this weird idea kept trying to creep in and make my stomach hurt. It felt like I was getting ready to face something I'd been avoiding a long time. But I wasn't as brave as Mark thought, because all I wanted to do was run away.

"Where are we going?" I asked.

It was the last day of winter break and we were on the bus again. Mark was taking me somewhere special before school started. He poked me in the ribs with his finger. "Quit it." I laughed. He poked me again and it made me squeal. A lady two rows up made a noise like she could go bulimic on all the flirting, but I didn't care. It was a perfect, warm, puffy-cloud day, despite the fact that it was January.

But as the bus wound through the residential streets again, it was like someone pulled a plug and all the giggles in me swirled down a drain and disappeared. When Mark got up at the same bus stop as last time, I resisted.

"Do you think this is a good idea?" I asked him.

"C'mon," he said. "We'll miss our stop."

Mark grabbed my hand and we walked the same way as before. Only in my mind, I'd hopped back on the bus and gone back to school. Two nights ago I'd been fantasizing that Mark and I got married, and horrifying myself with the idea I'd have to meet his mom again. It was bad enough to imagine it ten years in the future.

"Let's go to Salinas Street, huh?" I smiled at him, wondering who was working the controls for my face. "We could catch a movie."

"I want to show you something," he said. I had a crazy thought: *He doesn't remember last time*. I brushed it away. Of course he did. How could he forget?

"I don't think your mom . . ." I said. He tugged my hand again. I stayed where I was. Slowly, like he was forgetting I was there, he let go and walked up the path. He didn't look back. After a few seconds I followed him to the doorway.

The house was the same as before, except I could hear music from the kitchen. A Mark-sized guy stood in front of the fridge, drinking from a carton. Mark's brother, John, I figured. They studiously ignored each other. John shivered like a wet dog and shut the fridge door. Too much cold milk, I guessed.

"Hi," I began. But Mark tugged me into the living room, away from his brother.

"We don't get along," he whispered in my ear. He took me through the house to the hallway where their bedrooms were. Mark opened the door to the right again, the guest bedroom. I glanced in. His mother was asleep on top of the covers.

Next to me, the muscles in Mark's arm tensed. All the way down, like a series of goose bumps, until he was squeezing my fingers too tight again. I squeezed back.

Mrs. Elliott was curled up on the bed with her eyes closed, mascara all over her face. Like she'd cried herself to sleep. Her arms were folded up against her chest, holding a piece of clothing under her chin. Mark sat down next to her. The bedsprings creaked. He let go of my hand and gave her shoulder a little shake.

Mrs. Elliott opened her eyes and looked right at Mark. I wanted to bolt. Her eyes were red and bleary, and to be perfectly honest, she seemed a little out of it. But then she smiled. She uncrossed her arms and held out the cloth, like she was sharing a private joke with Mark. It was baby pajamas. Mark laughed. She grinned and a tear slid down the side of her nose. She opened her arms and Mark lay down next to her, his back to her chest. She nestled her face in his shoulder and closed her eyes.

If I were her kid and she treated me like she'd treated Mark that first time, I wouldn't have the guts to come back. But then again, there were probably a lot of things about their family I didn't understand. And snuggling infant clothes was on the top of that list.

Then it hit me: Maybe Mrs. Elliott had lost a baby. And then an even worse idea snuck into my head. Maybe Mark had been responsible, somehow. The thought punched me in the stomach. Was that why my boyfriend was exiled from his own home, why it was so painful for his mom to have him around? I didn't think I could ask him about something like that. My heart burst like a water balloon, flooding everything inside me with sadness.

I stumbled back to the kitchen. Mark's brother sat at the kitchen table, with a bowl of cereal.

"Hi," I said to him again.

I could see the tendons in his jaw working. That guy could shovel in the Cap'n Crunch. He grunted, although whether it was a greeting or part of his choking-down-food ritual, I couldn't be sure.

"Great day for the beach," I mumbled, wishing I were anywhere else that very moment. Actually, even arriving for an algebra final in my underwear sounded fantastic in comparison.

John scanned the room, like he was searching for the obnoxious bug pestering him with conversational tidbits. Like he wanted to swat me away but couldn't be bothered to look at me, I was so insignificant. Guess it was his way of letting me know his dislike of Mark meant I was persona non grata.

"Too cold in here." He dumped his half-eaten meal into the sink, spoon and all. I was trying to figure out a clever way to respond, something about it still being a great day outside the House of Awkward, but John walked away before I could say anything at all.

I stood there, thinking variants on the theme omigod-what-a-jerk! When I had done that to my satisfaction, my thoughts turned toward slipping out the front door. I wasn't too keen on waiting around while "Marky" had nap time with his mommy. I was kind of irritated that he'd just left me on my own. If Mark caught up with me at the bus stop, that was fine. Otherwise I'd see him at school.

My hand was on the doorknob when I heard shouting from the bedrooms upstairs. I didn't catch all of it, but this part echoed through the house loud and clear: "I'm the one who's still here!" It might have been Mark or John — that whole brother thing made it hard to tell. A second later, Mark ran past me. I stumbled on a throw rug, trying to get out of his way. When he opened the front door, it sounded like he cracked the frame. Like a sonic boom when it hit the back wall. Then he was gone. I heard sobbing upstairs. Their mother, I guessed.

I ran out, not so much chasing Mark as escaping as well. I didn't bother closing the door behind me. I just ran. It really was a great day outside. The sunlight was so bright gold and sparkly it blinded me. I didn't care. I ran blind.

CHAPTER 20

By the time I got back, campus was alive again. Kids dragged duffle bags like fat, little, legless sausage dogs behind them. Dorm lights that had been dark for two weeks glowed warm yellow through open windows.

There was no sign of Tamara in our room, but I could tell she was back, thanks to her unmade bed and clothes strewn across the floor. I was ready to flop onto my bed when I saw it, up on the shelf above Tamara's bed: this big, framed photo of Tamara, with her parents and older sister. Judging from how young Tamara was in it, the picture was an oldie but goodie. The whole family was squished together on a wide lawn, with big smiles and squinty eyes. It practically shouted in Tamara's annoying voice, "My parents love me!" It was just a stupid photo, I told myself. But it was more than I could take after watching Mark's family blow up. I tried to calm down. All those squinty, grinning faces leered at me. I could feel their smug, happy-family eyeballs searing into the back of my skull. How was I gonna live in this room and see that every day?

The next thing I knew, I was standing up there on Tamara's bed. I grabbed the picture off the shelf, ready to send it flying. But what I saw stopped me. There was Tamara stuff I'd never seen before on the shelf, like a secret hidden out in the open.

It wasn't a treasure trove or anything. A couple of shells and two pieces of sea glass. A bit of fine, brown baby hair tied with a lavender ribbon. A ripped red ticket stub admitting one. And another unframed photo lying flat.

I breathed out. Dust and sea-salt smells blew back in my face. The unframed photo showed two skinny adolescent boys with curly dark hair, smiling these sad smiles into the camera. Behind them, in the photo, white bedding and a little bit of stainless steel.

My legs got wobbly from trying to keep my balance on Tamara's lumpy mattress. I knew those guys in the picture. Except I didn't recognize them from school. At least I didn't think that was how I knew them. It was like a sneeze hitching around in my nose, trying to escape.

There was something under the photograph of the two boys. When I lifted it up, I could feel the dust on the photo getting into the ridges of my thumbprint. I think I must have known what it was going to be before I saw it, because for a second, I thought I was going to pass out.

Underneath the photo was the coin that Barnaby Charon had given me.

I stumbled back and hopped off the bed, my thumb still dusty from where I'd touched the photograph. *Tamara stole my coin.* I didn't know why it shocked me so bad. I mean, she'd been a sucky roommate to be sure, and I hated her and everything, and she probably didn't even know what that coin meant to me. But still, I could hardly believe that Tamara had gone into my closet and stolen it. It wasn't even my coin. It was Brynn's. I was furious. I was amazed I'd lucked out and found it. My brain didn't know which way to go.

I stumbled to my closet, knelt down, and put my hand into the toe of my black dress shoe. But there, where I'd hidden it, was the gold coin Barnaby Charon had given me. Not stolen at all. Even though I'd just seen it up there, with Tamara's junk. There were two coins. Counting the coin on Jessie's desk, maybe even three.

You remember who those boys in the picture were, right? my brain asked me. *Yeah*, I told myself right back. *They're the ones who snuck into our room that night. They're the boys Tamara said didn't exist.*

My roommate walked in, with Sasha the junior right behind her. Tamara was saying, "Omigod you will not believe what she said next. WILL. NOT. You will freak. You will totally, freaking die laughing." Tamara took her flip-flop off her foot and threw it to the floor to underline the freaking that was going to be happening.

"What?" Sasha was already laughing.

They both saw me at the same time and stopped mid-cackle. "Uh . . . Never mind," Tamara said. Her toe slipped back into her flip-flop. "I'll tell you later," she added, in a fake whisper, like I couldn't hear them a whole three feet away.

I flew out of the room, desperate to get away. Tamara's snotty "Was it something I said?" followed me out the door.

I went to Nora's room. She wasn't there, but her luggage was. I knew where to find her.

When I crawled into the secret room, she fumbled around for her penlight, turned it on, and set it on the floor. I was glad — alone in the dark was fine. Alone in the dark with another person was weird.

"You OK?" she asked. I nodded. And then, of course, I bawled. It was stupid, but the idea that I'd almost lost Brynn's coin had shaken me up. Or maybe it was just the cherry on top of the stress cake of what had happened with Mark. Whatever it was, it left me a blubbering mess.

"Oh, jeez." Nora sighed and sat next to me. I slumped over and she patted my back. She took a few strands of my hair and made braids. There was no Kleenex, so I wiped my nose with the front of my shirt.

"Attractive, huh?" I said.

"Yeah," she agreed. "You'd be a real catch for a guy with a mucus fetish."

I tried to laugh, but I kind of honked instead. Nora sat there and I sat there and she just waited, I guess, until I was ready. Then I told her what had happened with Mark's family. I told her about Tamara's coin. I told her about the picture of the boys. The words poured out of me like I was a widemouthed pitcher and someone tipped me until everything slipped right out and spilled everywhere. Finally I said, "I don't think I like Mark anymore." That was the last thing I had to say, because I waited and no more words came out.

"I had a bad vacation, too," Nora said.

"Yeah?" I was embarrassed to hear the hopeful tone in my voice. I guess I didn't want to be alone in having a complete disaster day. "What happened?"

She tugged on strands of my hair, twisting them into a careless design. I nudged her when she didn't answer me.

"Nothing," she said.

"Nothing happened?" I raised my eyebrow even though she couldn't see my face. She still didn't say anything. I reached over and grabbed the penlight. I was going to interrogate her, faux-cop style, pry out what had happened. Even though I was clearly going to win the gold, Nora could at least medal in the Sucky Winter Break Olympics.

"Drop it," she warned, pushing the light away. "I'm not ready to talk about it." Something in her voice was worse than unhappy. Whatever nothing had happened, it must have shaken her up.

"I got a permission slip from Mr. Graham," I said instead, remembering it at the exact same time as it came out of my mouth. "For the archives."

When Nora didn't say anything, I turned the tiny flashlight on her. In the small circle of light, she smiled. She was wearing a thin, old Rolling Stones T-shirt with a big tongue on the front. It had been washed and worn so many times the print was faded and peeling and the shirt itself was pretty much see-through. Anyone else would have retired it to jammies.

There was a Y-shaped, caterpillar-looking thing under her shirt, like a crazy, fuzzy, black necklace. Except when I saw it, I knew it was stitches. They went up each shoulder and met at her breastbone. The stitches themselves were uneven and thick — the kind they give you when you're not around to complain about what the scar is going to look like later. A little pinkish fluid blotted the Stones' emblem. It looked like Nora's bad vacation had been spent on an autopsy table.

I closed my eyes and thought about how maybe it was time to accept that I was losing my mind in a way that was more serious than a series of freak-outs caused by leaving home, or school pressure, or whatever else might explain it.

I heard faint knocking. *Let me in, Nora! Let me in!* It was a man, screaming, frantic. *Why did you lock the door?* The sound left shivers all down my arms. In my mind's eye, I saw a bathroom door shaking in its frame, clear as day. It wasn't locked. It wouldn't open because Nora was face-down on the floor in front of it.

Come back, reality, come back, I thought to myself. When I opened my eyes, Nora had no stitches.

It was like the returning students brought the January weather with them, because when Nora and I left the theater, darkness had fallen and a sharp chill had settled over campus. Nora took off to run laps under the lit track field, and I shivered all the way back to the dorms, the air cutting right through my thin lavender sweater.

It wasn't much warmer in our room. There was one thermostat for all of Kelser House. It was covered with a bubble of Plexiglas, and there was a big handwritten sign taped over it that said DO NOT ADJUST THERMOSTAT. I wasn't too worried about freezing, though, because everybody knew that Faye Rosen would be out there soon enough, with her nail file jammed between the wall and the edge of the Plexiglas, tickling the gauge over toward 80. Faye was a touch on the anorexic side, and those skinny chicks got two things fast: cold and cranky.

Tamara was in her bed, asleep, the covers pulled up under her armpits. I had half a mind to wake her up and yell at her about that picture I'd found. Proof that I had been right. I'd make her explain the coin, too. And I'd make her take down that smug family photo. I glared at it for a while before it occurred to me again that it was really an old photo. Not necessarily proof that Tamara had had fun over winter break. Only that, once upon a time, there had been a moment of goodness. Thinking that, I wasn't so bothered by their dumb smiles.

My mind kept turning back to the dust on the boys' photo. Maybe Tamara had her coin long before I got mine. I mean, she had already known who Barnaby Charon was when I asked her. *Keep him away from me*, she'd said.

Tamara's eyes fluttered in her sleep. Her lids peeled up, revealing two lines of white eyeballs. I heard Faye in the hallway, cursing. A minute later, the heater kicked on.

I sat at my desk for a while, thinking. Outside, there were occasional screams of laughter or shouts, but it was quieter than usual. On her side of the room, Tamara moaned in her sleep. It snapped me out of my thoughts, and I went to the bathroom to wash up. On my way back,

I noticed a piece of notebook paper folded and taped to my door. It had my name written in red pen on the front. Inside, it said:

> Come find me!
> —Brynn
> PS: I think I know what Jessie meant about the seat belt.

Brynn's room was empty. Where had she gone? Back in my room, I lay on top of my covers, worrying. But I must have fallen asleep, because I woke up the next morning, still wearing my clothes, on top of my bedcovers. Tamara was gone again.

The next afternoon, Nora and I presented our permission slip to Abby Claremont. She held the paper at arm's length, frowned, opened a drawer, and pulled out a set of keys. She marched us down the hallway and unlocked the door to the archives.

I guess I was expecting some huge thing, but it was just a

converted office with a bunch of books in it. No city of gold or Oompa-Loompas dancing around. To our left, a wall of yearbooks — bright ones with sharp spines at eye level, faded and rounded ones down on the bottom shelf.

When I opened one yearbook, it wasn't the standard mug-shot rows of freshmen, sophomores, or juniors. There were only pictures of maybe twenty students, identified as graduates. The seniors, I supposed, although a few of them looked pretty young. Each kid had a page detailing their accomplishments at Lethe. *We Will Miss You!* each page read. I closed the book.

Against the back wall, a couple of signs above the bookcases read LOCAL HISTORY and REFERENCE MATERIAL: DO NOT REMOVE FROM ROOM. A small wooden table and a single plastic chair were squeezed into the corner to our right. On the table, a clipboard. That was all there was. Well, except the stale smell of the place. If you ate nothing but old books and dust bunnies, this room would smell like your farts. I looked at Nora like, *Is this it?* But Nora wasn't interested in me.

"You need to sign in every time you use the archives." The librarian pointed to the clipboard. Nora signed her name without glancing down, already scanning titles in the reference section. Abby Claremont scowled at me, since Nora was apparently immune to her charms.

"You, too," she said. I picked up the clipboard. The page was three-quarters full of signatures. The dates went back fifteen years at the top of the page. I guessed it was a pretty exclusive place. I wrote my name. Mr. Graham's signature was above Nora's. It was from two weeks ago, the night of the winter formal. He must have come here after he'd signed our permission slip. There was no way to tell from the sheet what he'd done or found here. The librarian snatched the clipboard from me and cleared her throat.

"Thank you," Nora called, over her shoulder, all dismissive. After a final frown at Nora's back and my face, Ms. Claremont kicked the mounted doorstop down with her shoe.

"The door stays open," she said. I nodded. Nora might have forgotten the librarian existed.

When we were alone, Nora pulled some big, old books out of the reference section and hauled them over to the table.

"What are you trying to find?" I asked her.

"Huh?" she said. It occurred to me that I had also probably ceased to exist in her world.

"Now that we made it here, what are you searching for?"

"Information about the coin and other stuff," she mumbled, nose in a book already. Without wanting to, I reached into my pocket and touched Brynn's danake. I no longer kept it in my shoe. The idea of not having it on me made me super-uncomfortable.

"Like what?" I asked.

"Look," Nora said. "I can tell you what I'm doing, or I can do it." She added, "I don't know what's going on. It makes me mad to try and explain something when I don't understand it."

Nora wouldn't look me in the eye. I stood there, not sure what to do. Finally I gave up — as with her vacation, she'd tell me when she was ready.

"I'm off like a dirty shirt," I said.

"Mmm-hmm." Nora was back in the book already. She rubbed her collarbone with her fingertips as she read, and I could almost make myself hallucinate stitches again. Like they were under her skin, scratching her.

I headed for the dining hall to get something to eat, wondering why Nora was acting so wary and what Brynn's note meant. I was halfway inside my own head as I marched out of the kitchen with my food and looked for a seat. Mark sat at the far end of the dining hall, eating with Beau. They were in tennis whites, and they were laughing about something.

Mark wolf-whistled when he saw me, and I felt myself go completely red. I'd been avoiding him since he'd come back to campus. My brain was still angry enough not to want to like the guy anymore, but my heart? *I'm in love with him*, I realized as I looked at him across the cafeteria. It knocked me back in my shoes a little.

I didn't know you could love someone and be so mad you couldn't stand them at the same time. *Yes, you did*, a small part of me whispered. *Because of Lia.*

It must have been the stress from everything, but as I stood there holding my tray, tears welled up in my eyes, and I couldn't help grinning like an idiot. When Mark waved me over to sit with him, no angry part of my brain could talk me out of going over and giving him the biggest hug ever.

I was more floating than walking when I went through the breezeway between the faculty room and the Rowntree

Room after dinner. Mr. Graham stood with his back to me, studying the sign-up sheet for the spring fling cruise. Most of me was still back in the dining hall, basking in the sunshine of Mark's attention.

"Give me Brynn's coin," he said, as I passed by, almost under his breath. He turned to face me. The skin under his eyes was pale, like he'd been crying, and his nose was red. That cowlick at the back of his head was standing up again, angry-rooster style.

"What?" My brain was a little slow to understand what he'd said. My body knew right away. In second grade, Lia had dared me to chew a piece of tinfoil. The coin zinged my leg like that.

I took it out of my pocket and opened my palm to show him. Mr. Graham stared at it for a long time, his head bent so I couldn't see his face. Every time he breathed out, warm air tickled my fingertips. I didn't mind. Showing the coin to someone else felt like a confession. He reached out until his hand hovered over mine, but he stopped and never got any closer.

He said, "I can't take hers. No matter what I do, I can only take one for myself."

Anyone could see the guy was struggling not to cry, so I was surprised when he laughed.

"Are you sure this coin doesn't belong to you?" he asked. A shred of hopefulness twisted across his face. I didn't know what he was *really* asking, but I did know the answer. I shook my head. He clenched his fist in the air above my hand, until his knuckles went white and he said, "No. I know it's for her."

"What do you know?" I asked.

"Your lips are purple." He swallowed when he said it. Like whatever he meant to say was far more horrible than how it sounded. My mind's eye flashed to Nora's caterpillar stitches, but as soon as I thought it, I shook the connection off. My lips probably *were* purple. Everything on me felt numb-clammy cold and I'm sure it showed on my face. I rubbed my hand across my mouth.

"You went to the archives," I said. It came out like an accusation. He turned away, the hand that couldn't take the coin still clenched at his side. "What do you know?" I demanded, as he walked off. My voice bounced around, amplified and echoing back at me. Mr. Graham stopped, but he didn't turn back to me.

"Charon will end you when he finds out you've been in there," he said, over his shoulder. "Your friend, too." Then he was gone.

A teacher at my school couldn't possibly have told me another adult was going to harm me. I stuffed the coin back in my pocket. It wasn't easy, because my hand was shaking pretty bad. A crazy thought fell into my head like a quarter in a slot machine and hit jackpot, with ideas falling out all over the place.

Those stitches I'd seen on Nora weren't a hallucination. They were a premonition. If I didn't do something, Barnaby Charon was going to end Nora. Not expel her from school, not put her on work crew until the end of time, but end her life.

When I got back to the library, Nora was already gone, the archives room locked up like it had never been opened. I didn't knock when I got to her bedroom, just threw the door open and saw it was empty.

My brain was like a blender on high speed, and all the stuff I knew whirled around. Probably, Nora had found something about Barnaby Charon in that archives room.

But what? A confession note? A job application where Barnaby Charon listed "serial killer" under his previous occupations? Plus, how could Mr. Graham know and not do anything?

I sprinted to the dorm bathrooms and called out her name, then ran past the common room. "Nora!" I yelled.

"Shut up," someone from behind a closed door replied.

I ran back up the hill and checked the dining hall. No Nora. No one had seen her and no one had any idea where I might find her. Maybe she was with Brynn. Trying to figure out the location of any given teenager on campus over the weekend? Might as well get yourself a cowboy hat and take up cat herding. I mean, you'd be less frustrated.

I ran toward the faculty room to tell whatever adults I found what had happened. I was halfway there before I slowed down to a walk. What was I going to do — repeat what Mr. Graham had said? Even if they wanted to believe me, it was only a vague, secondhand threat coming from a teacher. They wouldn't be looking for Barnaby Charon. They'd be looking for Mr. Graham. I stopped and closed my eyes and breathed until I knew where I was supposed to go.

When I pulled open the heavy doors, the theater was deserted. I fished out my key to the secret room and scanned the seats and stage, making sure I was alone. Above my head, a red EXIT sign glowed. Nora had to be up in the secret room, waiting for me, safe behind the locked door she'd made. I took a few steps inside.

Behind me, the theater doors swung open again. I jammed the key into my pocket and turned, hoping to see Nora. Or Brynn. Thatch. Maybe Mr. Cooper.

It was Barnaby Charon.

Neither of us moved. The memory of his fingers around my throat was so strong I could hardly breathe. This was trouble. Could I outrun him? Maybe. I was fast and I was scared and I wasn't some stupid girl in a horror movie who'd trip over her own shoes. At least, I hoped I wasn't that girl.

But then Barnaby Charon grabbed my wrist, his hands all bones and leathery skin, and yanked me into the gloaming of the theater. *That's the end, then*, I thought. *Should have taken my chance while I had it.*

"It is time for you to deliver the coin," he said.

"I don't have it," I lied.

"Will you be broken, then, like bread?" he asked. I thought: *Better to go down fighting. Better to* . . . "Let us check." He stuck his other hand into my front pocket and pulled it inside out. I screamed. The sound came out all reedy and powerless and flickery, like a cheap birthday candle. *Yell, dummy! Or he's going to kill you!* I thought. My voice cracked and then came out loud and clear and strong. I yelled until my ears rang and I had to take a big, whooping breath to scream again.

"You freaking monster!" I shouted at him, which was not exactly the international distress call I'd been expecting, but it was what came out of me. Charon started reaching into my other pocket, evidently not caring that I was yelling and twisting and kicking his shins. The doors opened behind us. We both froze.

"I knew you'd be here." Brynn stood under the glow of the EXIT light, watching us. Like it was no big thing to walk in on a kid being mauled by an adult.

"Go get help!" I yelled. Then I bit Barnaby Charon. Right on the hand that held me. It didn't seem to bother him. I could have been a two-year-old having a temper tantrum.

Brynn limped toward us, which was totally the wrong way to go for help. Her eyes focused on Charon.

"I am the help," she said.

Brynn stepped closer. I twisted as best as I could, searching the rest of the theater for someone to save us, because it didn't seem like Brynn was going to cut it.

"Silence." Charon gave me a shake, making my teeth chatter together. He sounded somehow both cheerful and annoyed. To Brynn he said, "It is your time. This creature has your coin. She was instructed to give it to you, but disobeyed. Come and get it, if you dare."

"Let her go," Brynn said. He did. I fell on my butt, crying and still screaming a little bit. All my systems were go for freak-out. Out of the corner of my eye, I saw a glimmer of gold as that stupid coin he'd been searching for bounced on the floor next to us.

"She kept the coin, hoping she could protect you. Foolish, yes?" Barnaby Charon asked Brynn, with a sly smile.

"I know what you are. I called you here," Brynn said to him, her voice shaking.

"I could take her instead." Charon tipped his head toward me, his tone menacing. He was trapping Brynn somehow, I could tell. I saw her waver. "Make no mistake — I will come back for you. But leave us now, pretend you saw nothing, and let Camden go in your place." He struck a bargaining tone. "In exchange, you will have another day at Lethe. But if I'm forced to release her, do not doubt I will take you instead."

"Brynn, run!" I screamed.

She looked so afraid I was sure she'd bolt. Instead, she straightened her spine and stood her ground. "Let. Her. Go," Brynn answered. It was like thunder cracking, like she was some superhuman. *I am your friend*, she might have said in the echo.

For a moment, the room went white as lightning, bleaching out my retinas, melting away my ability to see Brynn and Barnaby Charon. Panic pushed me to my feet and I scrambled, half-blind, for the far exit. I ran for a thousand years and got only a little bit closer.

"Hey! Are you OK?" I was so surprised to hear a new voice behind me, I turned midstep, blinking wildly. Thatch stood alone, next to the other exit. No sign of Barnaby Charon or Brynn anywhere.

And sure enough, just exactly like one of those dumb horror-movie girls, I tripped over my own feet and fell. Thatch jogged over.

"You OK?" he asked again, and held out his hand to help me up.

"Barnaby Charon," I said. "Did you see him? Did he have Brynn?"

"Did I scare you?" Thatch seemed kind of foolishly pleased with himself.

Running back to where the three of us had stood, I shoved open the other door and looked out. Nothing but deep twilight and the sound of crickets outside — no people at all. I sprinted down to the stage. Nothing. Except for me and Thatch, the theater was empty. Barnaby Charon and Brynn had disappeared.

Adrenaline made my mouth sour, and my heart loped around like a deer that'd been nicked by a bullet. I ran back to Thatch. "Barnaby Charon was here with Brynn." I spun around, searching for the danake. It wasn't anywhere.

"Oh," Thatch said. He pointed his finger at me and laughed. "Hey, you dropped your pocket."

Both my front pockets were turned out, showing white cotton and, in the corner of the left one, a ball of blue lint. "What?" I asked.

Thatch waved the idea away with his hand. "We used to say that all the time, right? Because you can't drop a pocket."

I stared at him.

"Take it easy," Thatch called, as I left.

CHAPTER 21

I sprinted to the faculty room, the torn-up shreds of what had happened trying to sew themselves into a whole cloth of a story. I rounded the corner of the breezeway and stopped short. Mr. Cooper stood at the threshold of the faculty room. The door was half-open behind him.

"Brynn!" I was breathing so hard from running that I could only cough the word out. I pointed with both index fingers at my inside-out pockets, like I was some crazy gunslinger, or like I thought the pockets could do my explaining for me. Mr. Cooper's face didn't change, so I said, "Barnaby Charon attacked me. He took Brynn."

Behind him, back in the faculty room, glass broke. Mr. Cooper closed his eyes at the sound. I pushed my way past the drama teacher. But instead of me going in, Mr. Graham walked out, his face that ashy white you mostly see on people right after they've tossed their cookies.

"I let her go to him," he said. "I didn't try to stop her."

A tear slid down Mr. Cooper's face, but he smiled. "I know, Henry."

"He was going to *end* me." I shoved Mr. Graham right in the chest. "Just like you said. Just like — and Brynn . . ." I tried to put together what had happened. "Brynn went instead. Brynn protected me." Barnaby Charon had asked me, "Will you be broken, then?" I flashed to Jessie's Ouija board, broken as well. Had Barnaby Charon used me to set Brynn up, somehow? He'd given her a choice. Brynn had gone, and she'd taken her danake. I kind of lost my mental footing, wondering if all that was true. Finally, I decided it was. "He's got her. Please. Do something." I shoved him again for emphasis.

"Camden," Mr. Cooper said, in a voice that was gentle and quiet. "It can't be helped."

A bleating, throbbing sound started up in my head. I pushed past the two worthless teachers and went into the faculty room, searching for someone who could do something. There was no one in the room except me. I picked up the phone on the desk, wondering if the ringing was someone calling. There was nothing but dial tone when I put the receiver to my ear. A broken picture frame lay on the floor next to the desk. Glass shards made triangles and diamonds and stardust and a tiny cluster of galaxies on the wood floor. The picture itself was gone, but I knew what it was, because I had seen the frame before. It was the one of Mr. Graham and his little sister, and it had broken when I'd stood in the hallway and said Brynn was gone. He must have brought it with him. In my mind's eye, I could see him holding it to his chest, just like my keeping Brynn's danake close. "I let her go," Mr. Graham had said.

A cold feeling came over me, that whatever was going to happen to Brynn had already been done. The idea set in my head like concrete, and I stood for a long time, staring at the pretty pieces of glass.

When I walked back to the doorway, Mr. Cooper was still there. "Help me," I said to him, even though he had never been any bit of use in all the time I had known him. He pointed to the wall, at the flyer Mr. Graham had been studying that morning. It said:

SPRING FLING CRUISE SIGN-UP SHEET
HOSTED BY: BARNABY CHARON, CAPTAIN

And the names, written in the same hand:

Jessie Keita
Troy Davis
Brynn Laurent
Nora Alpert
Henry Graham

Fear wormed its way through my insides. *It only looks like a sign-up sheet*, I thought. But it felt like a secret message, perhaps solely for me. It also felt like a good-bye.

Sad, scared loneliness overwhelmed me, like I'd been playing hide-and-seek in a graveyard, and everyone had been found but me. The bottom of the sheet read: *Nueva Vista Yacht Club, Pier 1*. But there was no time or date for the meet-up, just a map showing how to get there.

I was scared to go back to the theater, but I knew I had to, because of Nora. Because the Nora I knew would never agree to go on a cruise with Barnaby Charon. And mostly because Nora would have come and found me by now.

I opened the theater door and stood in the doorway,

half in and half out of the building, for a long time. Barnaby Charon did not return. I finally realized that if he wanted me, he would have taken me instead of Brynn. Or with Brynn. I mean, what he was doing probably wasn't like fishing, where you could only catch your limit and then you had to throw the rest back.

So I got my guts set and crept into the building, past the stage, and up the narrow stairway behind the velvet curtain. In a few more steps, I stood in front of the entrance to the secret room. I took out my key and crawled into the tunnel. I turned the corner, feeling my shoulders rub against both walls. When I got to the door Nora had constructed, I fumbled around, holding the key in one hand while I felt for the padlock with my other. It was already unlocked. As my eyes adjusted, I saw it was more than unlocked. Nora's makeshift door was broken, cracked, and splintered down the center, one hinge ripped out of the wood, the metal twisted from the force of whatever had happened.

"Nora!" I whispered. No one answered. I listened and listened and listened and didn't hear anything, not even phantom knocking. Then I went in.

The secret room was dark and silent. The only sign of life was the uneven sound of my breathing. I fumbled around on my hands and knees until I found the penlight. In the zigzag stripes of light, I saw that Nora wasn't there, and that was good, because when I'd called her name and she hadn't answered, I'd been afraid she was lying on the floor inside, dead. I sat down and watched the light jitter on the wall until my shakes got smaller and smaller and the light got steady.

There were books on the floor. Nora must have stolen them from the archives. They were all open and piled one on top of another. She must have been up here, studying them. Whatever she had read had made her leave the splintered wreckage of her door unlocked behind her. Even though I was pretty sure I didn't want to see, my body had its own plan. I sank down to my knees in front of the books Nora had left.

The one on top was opened to a big, glossy photo. It was an oil painting of half-naked people piling into a wooden boat docked on black water. The oarsman stood in rags. Underneath the picture, it said: *Nineteenth-Century Interpretation of Charon's Crossing.*

On the opposite page, I read: *Charon, the mythological ferryman on the river Styx, carried the newly deceased from the land of the living to the land of the dead. . . .*

I pushed the book away. It slid off the top of the pile.

The one underneath was an encyclopedia. The entry on the open page read: *Psychopomps are mediators between conscious and unconscious realms. Their purpose is not to judge the souls, but to protect them on their journey into the afterlife.*

The next book read: *Forms of obolos: payment for passage across the river Styx.* Underneath that heading were dozens of grainy, black-and-white photographs of coins, each with its own subtitle. Two rows down, I found the coin Barnaby Charon had given me: *Danake, gold (Persian).* At the bottom of the page, the text continued. *Those who died without an obol were required to wander the shore for a hundred years. . . .*

I pushed it away, too. On the bottom of the pile, one more book was open to more paintings of Charon crossing the river Styx. In the paintings, there was always a dark figure escorting scared, sad-looking people onto an overgrown canoe. The image of Charon was skeletal, blurred, vague, and anonymous.

But there, sitting in the boat. I recognized *that* guy, despite the toga and old-time flip-flops. The passenger wore the same tear-streaked face I'd seen up in the faculty room. Our drama teacher, Mr. Cooper.

"You knew who Barnaby Charon was all along," I whispered at his image.

It was the craziest thing, but all I could think of was how the ringing in my head had stopped and how quiet everything was, up here in the dark. And that's when I knew why Nora had gone. The others, too. I threw the book across the room. It hit Nora's broken door and crumpled to the floor, like a bird hitting a window, pages fluttering.

Broken. I thought of Jessie's broken Ouija board. What about the picture frame in the faculty room? That had been Mr. Graham's — the picture of his sister. What about Nora's door?

Everything broken was something important to that person, I guessed. Although exactly how it worked, I didn't understand. Maybe those things had to be destroyed for the people to get their coins. Had I been Brynn's important thing? I must have been, since I'd given up her coin. Except I didn't feel broken. What happened with Brynn in the theater made me feel changed for sure, but not destroyed like the Ouija board.

I crawled out of the secret room, not caring how loud I was. I left the broken door behind me, with the books still open for whoever needed them next. I was ready to meet Barnaby Charon. I knew the directions to find him were back on the spring fling cruise sign-up sheet. The only problem was that I needed payment for the guy, and I still couldn't figure out what I needed to break to get my coin. Then I realized I had already broken something.

I went to the squash courts. It was full dark outside by then. The security lights were on, and the pay phone stood in a pool of illumination next to the locker rooms. As I walked up to it, it felt exactly right. This was the place where I had both been broken and broken something. I took a deep breath and jammed my finger into the coin return.

The thing was, I was so sure of what I was going to find that I was practically on my way before I realized there was nothing between my fingers. I bent over, poked the little metal door aside, and peered into the darkness of the coin return. Nothing was in there. Very slowly, I straightened, holding on to the phone booth, where my dad had told me I couldn't come home. For a crazy moment, I wondered if maybe I had the wrong phone. Or the wrong idea.

I grabbed the phone and put it to my ear. "Dad?" I asked. Nothing but a dial tone. The phone stood there, being nothing more than an ordinary phone in front of me.

"I didn't want you to have it," Mark said. I hung up and

turned around. He stood there, trying to smile, watching me like I might be dangerous. It made my skin prickle and tingle to have him look at me like that. "It fell out of the return when I hung the phone up. I put my shoe on it when you started crying." He stepped forward with one foot, mimicking what he had done.

"You still have it," I said.

He shook his head no.

The air in my lungs froze into a block of ice that I couldn't blow out or suck all the way in. Then, very slowly, Mark nodded. And like that, I could breathe again.

"I need it." I held out my hand. I had a boat to catch.

"No, you don't, Cam." He stuffed his hands in his jeans pockets, and I knew he had brought the coin with him, just as I had started carrying Brynn's around. He stepped back. "You can't just . . ." He looked away. "Everyone else leaves. You should stay here with me."

"I know about Charon," I said. I opened my mouth to tell him — I had a crazy idea for a second that we could go together.

"Don't!" he yelled at me. "I don't want to know what you know."

"But . . ."

"I heard what your dad said to you." He stepped closer and touched my arm. "You are worth something to *me*. I would never want you to leave."

What he said fluttered around in my ribcage like a living bird. Even if Mark didn't understand everything, I knew what he was asking me to do. I stepped closer. His breath tickled the side of my neck, and I knew all those little secrets you know about another person when they are very close, like the smell of his toothpaste and deodorant, even the detergent in his clothes. I tried to put every small detail of him into my head, so I could keep them forever.

"Please," he said, his voice hoarse. "It will break me to let you go."

A flicker of understanding lit up my mind, about why I'd had Brynn's coin, and maybe why Mark had mine. I slipped my hand around his neck and pulled his face down to mine, so we were breathing the same air.

"It doesn't break you. I think it heals you." It was my coin, not his. The thing that had to break was my heart.

He whispered, "You stood up that day in the chapel. Fearless. I dream about it sometimes."

"I love you," I told him, as he leaned down to kiss me.

For an answer, he slid his hand between us and opened his fist. I took the coin.

From Little Quad Lawn, I watched Mr. Graham's motorcycle circle the parking lot, gain speed, and finally rev up the hill. The wind blew my hair back as he slowed to a stop next to me. I said, "I need to go to the marina. Can you take me there?"

Mr. Graham wiped his eyes like a little kid and gave me a sad smile. "Hop on."

As he drove, faster and faster, I became a bird, flying low over the crest of the mesa and past the gates of Lethe. In a blur, I saw that strange little meadow. It was certainly a graveyard, and I was escaping it.

Down through the canopy of trees, then the rows of blossoming orange trees, we rode through town and to the darkness of the yacht club pier, where Mr. Graham brought the motorcycle to a purring stop and let me off.

"Are you sure?" he asked. When I nodded, he said, "This you do alone." I turned for only a moment, just to see if Barnaby Charon was there. But that was all it took. When I glanced back over my shoulder, Mr. Graham was gone.

CHAPTER 22

When I met him at the ocean's edge, I wasn't scared. The sea was black as ink under the night sky, lapping and gurgling against the dock posts, taunting me. But the water wouldn't end my life. He would. A smile flickered across his face, like he could read my thoughts.

Barnaby Charon was alone, standing in the darkness on the pier. There was a building out there, and he stood next to it. Inside, the lights were off and the glass of the windows reflected the ocean. I thought we were the only two people left on earth.

I took a deep breath.

"How long have I been dead?" I asked him.

CHAPTER 23

"Usually, by the time a person meets with me, they have completely passed," he said. I thought back to the first time I had ever laid eyes on Barnaby Charon. I had been dead since before Denver, apparently.

"Usually passed," I said. "But not always?"

He nodded. "If you will, recall the touch we shared on the airplane."

I knew what he was talking about, but the way it went down in my memory was not so much a "touch we shared," as him grabbing my neck. I had thought he was going to kiss me, but . . .

"You were checking my pulse," I realized.

"You had none." He smiled out to sea, like he was fond of the memory.

That's right about when it sunk in. I mean, technically,

I had known since I had seen Nora's books, but the knowing was on top of my brain, like a hat I was wearing. When he smiled, the knowing sunk down into me like syrup into a pancake. My knees got wobbly and I wanted to sit down, but the dock looked dank. *You'll get your clothes dirty*, my head kept trying to tell me. Except that wasn't true — ghosts, or dead people, or whatever — they didn't need to worry about that stuff anymore. But that wasn't exactly right, either, because here I was, dead, and I was still worried about it.

The light came on in the building next to us. Through a window, I saw it was a yachtsman's clubhouse. It looked warm and inviting, with a polished wood bar, and twinkly glasses that hung from the ceiling, and comfy-looking yellow chairs with navy stripes.

"Let us go inside." He walked ahead to get the door. In the moonlight, I saw the shine of his hair go white and smooth and skull-like.

Inside, I fell into a chair. Charon went to the bar and made himself a drink. The glasses behind him were etched with the names of poisons. His had "strychnine" on it. I was pretty sure that was a joke. Charon half sat on a bar stool and sipped his drink.

"What happens when you take me across the water?" I asked.

"It is my purpose to take you there. When you are ready." He hadn't exactly answered my question. "First, there is something you must do," he added.

I tensed up. If I was already dead, what could he want from me? I could feel a pull inside my chest, like he had my heart on a leash and he could yank me wherever it was he meant for me to go.

I asked, "What is this place? How did I end up here?"

"The school is a way station. It is a place for you to process what has happened and a chance to get your affairs in order before you pass into the next realm. Those who die young or suddenly often have unfinished business. Every student must fulfill two requirements. One is understand that you have died. Receiving a coin is the mark of understanding."

He leaned across the bar and reached for something. Then he walked over and placed a book in my lap as if it weighed nothing at all, even though it was as big as a dictionary. The cover was oiled by a million fingerprints.

I expected the thing in my lap to be like a baby book, a *This Is Your Life, Camden*. But the first page was an obituary for Jake Diaz, a junior guy I hardly even knew. I flipped more pages. The whole book was full of newspaper clippings of my schoolmates. Sometimes it was a little blurb of an article, like with Jake, who'd been in a car accident. Or it was like the next article, which had a small paragraph under the headline *Family of Four Dead in Home: Carbon Monoxide Likely Culprit*. Sometimes they were big articles on old, yellowed, and crackly paper. Others looked new.

I saw my prank buddy, Rachel, smiling in an old holiday card. Next to her photo, the words: *House Fire Claims Victim*. Followed by, *Firefighters were called to the 1800 block of North Kingston Street Wednesday afternoon. There, they rescued sixteen-year-old Rachel Smith from the burning home. She later died at the hospital. Authorities suspect faulty wiring. . . .* I studied it for a long time, trying to believe it and failing.

I turned the page. *Two Minors Perish in Rollover Accident*. It read, *Both victims were pronounced dead at the scene.* Next to the article was the photo I'd seen on Jessie's desk, of her and her brother.

"She thought she lived through that crash with her brother." I remembered what Jessie told me. "But she knew there was something wrong with her seat belt."

Charon said, "The brain obscures the events of death. It is the last survival instinct."

"What do you mean — what does that mean?" I demanded of Professor Death over there, with his fifty-cent college words.

"Jessie believed she survived the accident because she *had* worn her seat belt, but she did not. The argument with her brother distracted both from their tasks. The mind is cleverer than the person: It can both know the truth and obscure it until the person is prepared to face what has happened to them. Jessie suffered tremendous guilt, believing her speech impediment prevented her brother from fastening his seat belt. The only words she was able to say clearly were 'I hate you.' Seeking out her brother with the Ouija board, she was able to forgive herself. So absolved, she awoke to her true existence and then knew to call for me."

"You took her." I slumped down. I had known, of course. But I had thought he killed her.

He seemed the slightest bit offended. "I only supplied the vehicle. She drove herself."

"Why . . . ?" I started, but I knew. Just as I met Charon down by the water's edge, Jessie had come here in a car like the one that had killed her.

In that moment, I understood that the spring fling cruise had been only for me, a sign telling me where I needed to go.

"Did Jessie really talk to her brother that night in the chapel?" I asked instead.

"Yes. The dead may speak across realms to other dead."

A horrible idea crossed my mind — I'd called my father. "What about the living? Can you contact them?" My chest got tight. I thought I might die all over again if I found out my dad was dead.

"Your father dreams of you. He slept, aching with loss, when you called," Charon said.

"He misses me?" I asked. Charon leaned over and handed me a soft linen handkerchief. His face suggested he was trying hard not to show it, but maybe, buried deep under the thousands of years of doing this job, he was still a little grossed out by human things like snot leakage. I wiped my nose.

"You are his daughter."

"He said I couldn't come home," I whispered.

"Of course he did. You are dead. You cannot." Charon smiled a little. "Haunting is a seductive and destructive force within every deceased. It has the great potential to damage both you and the ones you attempt to contact. It distracts from the tasks that must be completed in this realm. Your father knew this. His was an act of great love to discourage your return."

I thought about my dad telling me not to come home. Not because he didn't want me, but because he loved me. Because he was still trying to do right by me, even though he probably thought I was a figment of his dreams. Charon had just told me that it was bad — a haunting — but all I wanted to do right then was call my dad again and tell him I loved him. *I'm not a figment*, I'd say, and he'd know it was me. I closed my eyes. I could call every day and tell him I loved him, and maybe after a while, it would be like I wasn't even dead, and everything would be OK, and . . .

Except I knew what that looked like. I'd seen it first-hand at Mark's house.

"Some kids get lost when they try to go back home, don't they?" The book in my lap was warm, like a sleeping cat, and I turned the page without waiting for him to answer.

The obituary was only a small column. No bold head-line or picture, just life and death news in a small town: *Mark Elliott, eight months, passed away in his home in Nueva*

Vista of Sudden Infant Death Syndrome (SIDS). He is survived by his parents, Edward and Nancy, and his brother, John.

"Mark isn't a baby," I said.

"This is haunting," Charon said. "Sometimes he stays with your kind, he grows and learns. Sometimes he gets caught up in contact with his past." His face hardened the slightest bit. "He will not see me."

"Was that his mother I saw? And his brother?" I got an icky feeling in my stomach. "Did *I* haunt them?"

"To them, if they felt you at all, you were an unwelcome presence. An eerie sensation."

"A ghost?" I asked.

Charon shrugged. "As a mother whose heart is still broken for him, Nancy is able to recognize Mark. In her grief, she can neither hold on to her son nor let him go."

"She wants him to come back to her," I said. "Even though she says she doesn't."

"Who knows what a human heart wants?" His eyes burned, the color of the liquor in his strychnine glass.

"Will he ever . . . ?" I thought about what Mark had said to me the last time I'd seen him: "I don't want to know what you know." I shut my mouth. I opened it again and asked before I could think it through: "Will he ever get what he needs from his mom? You know, so he can pass?"

"Attend to what I have told you. He requires nothing from his mother. The one Mark must make peace with is his brother."

Like I was right back in their spooky, haunted house, I heard Mark's brother scream: "I'm the one who's still here!" John wouldn't have his mother back until Mark let her go. And maybe Mark had lost too much of her to let go of the shreds he still had.

"But . . . wait," I said, stumbling in my head over it. "How can Mark be haunting his mom — and that's bad — but he's still supposed to talk to John to do whatever it is he's supposed to do? Wouldn't that be haunting his brother?"

"Ah." Charon sipped his drink. "There is haunting and there is visitation. The former involves your neediness and desire to be healed, and as I said, it damages. The latter involves your ability to deliver healing to the one you contact. A visitation is a gift to another that may damage you."

Charon set his drink down, and I watched a blue flame skate across the surface of the liquid inside. It snuffed out and the drink was just a drink again.

I sat there with my mouth hanging half open, until

all the big words he'd used kind of filtered through and I thought I knew what he meant. But also, another part of me was back at school, by the telephone with Mark. "He had my coin," I whispered.

"Some students are charged with holding the coin of another, when the lessons are intertwined. You were able to show Mark that it is possible to love someone and also let them go, without being destroyed by the process. Before you, he was unable to contemplate it, but it is the skill he must gain to free himself of Lethe."

"What about me? What was my lesson?" I swallowed back tears.

"That you are capable of both loving someone and knowingly hurting them. As all people are. Mark will ache from your decision, and you knew this, and you chose your coin, anyway."

I nodded, my heart heavy. I closed my eyes and went back to that moment at the pay phone. Except this time, somehow I did something differently, which changed things. I would take that coin, pinch it between my fingers, and push it right back in the coin slot. I would hear it chink down into the belly of the pay phone, and then I'd grab Mark's hand and . . .

"What if . . ." Trying to explain that you love someone is no easy thing. The best I could get out after a while was "Please."

The boatman's jaw set. "You cannot save him from pain. You cannot even save yourself."

I couldn't have stayed at Lethe, knowing what I did. But part of me wanted to. When no words showed up to explain how it felt, all these tears came out instead.

Charon studied the ocean.

I turned the page of the book in my lap. It occurred to me that each obituary got me closer to my own page. I tried to get lost in the little articles and updates, understanding these secrets about the people I had known on campus. There was Thatch, who was riding a bike when he got hit by a car. In a way, it was overwhelmingly sad to see death everywhere. But in another way, it made me smile. I mean, I knew how Thatch turned out — he'd gotten to kiss a girl like Nora. Death wasn't the end of him.

A few pages later, I saw Troy had died during a frat initiation party, of alcohol poisoning. I bet he knew all about peer pressure. Then I thought about what he'd said to me after Brynn's egging. I didn't have to ask — I knew he must've spied a gold coin swimming in the yolk of his last broken egg. It gave me chills to know I'd been so close to someone else's crossing over, and I hadn't even known it.

Next I saw: *Two Men Found Dead, One Missing.* The first paragraph read, *The bodies of Alan Wentz and Shane Stanton, both twenty-five, were found Monday in Los Padres National Forest, at the bottom of a ravine. Forensics suggests horseplay was likely a contributing factor in their deaths.*

"They were older in their . . . article . . . than they were at school," I said.

Shrug. "Sometimes you go backward to learn what you need to go forward," he answered. I thought about what bullies they were, what they'd done to Brynn.

"What happened to them?" I asked.

"Does it matter to you?" Charon answered. It was not a question. It felt good to let them go. *Good-bye, jerks*, I thought.

Brynn was next. *Teen Tennis Champ Missing*, the first headline announced in bold font. *The missing girl was last seen leaving Feather Point Country Club with her mother's former boyfriend, Ned Dillinger. . . .* Then: *Jenni Laurent Alibis Ned Dillinger in Daughter's Disappearance.* Followed by: *No Body? No Trial? No*

Justice for Brynn. And the last one: *FOUND!* It was next to a grainy photo of Brynn smiling in her tennis whites.

The mystery of Brynn Laurent's disappearance ended last month, when cold-case detectives found her remains buried on the property of oil executive Ned Dillinger. Authorities had long suspected Dillinger, the on-again, off-again boyfriend of Brynn's mother, Jenni Laurent. Several witnesses claimed Dillinger had a "creepy" interest in the teenager. Laurent alibied Dillinger, but suspicions were raised when Dillinger later purchased several luxury items for Laurent, including a house on Wedgewood Drive and a Lexus convertible.

Charon smiled. "Every student has a mortal wound. An injury that is echoed throughout their time here, until it is resolved. Tell me, what was Brynn's?"

I felt sick, trying to imagine what kind of mother Jenni Laurent must have been. And then, of course, I thought about how Brynn had gotten egged. "People who were supposed to care for her used her."

Charon nodded. "The thing that has damaged you, Camden, is the thing you must face."

The shadow of how this theory might apply to me slunk into my ear and hung out in the back of my brain. Examining it would have been like squeezing a tube of understanding toothpaste — there'd be no going back once it was out, and I got the feeling it was going to make a big mess, too. I shook my head, my short hair brushing against my neck.

"Is that what happened in the theater?" I asked.

He nodded. "Jenni Laurent once stumbled upon Brynn at the hands of a terrifying ghoul, much as Brynn discovered you and me in the theater. That woman turned a blind eye, forfeiting her daughter for her own selfishness. To receive her coin, Brynn had to do what her mother could not. She refused to sacrifice you, and broke free of becoming like her own mother."

"Why did I have her coin?" I asked.

Charon's voice turned sharp. "Do not ask that to which you know the answer." He tapped the center of his chest, where a person's heart would be, and I knew. Brynn and I, we'd learned how to be friends. When Charon's finger pressed the linen of his shirt, I saw the smooth bones of his ribcage. His finger tapped once more and then turned and pointed at me. I blotted away tears.

"Mr. Graham knew what you were, and he knew I had Brynn's coin. Why didn't he try and save her?" I asked. But then I remembered Mr. Graham told me: *I let her go.* Mr. Graham's obituary was next: a motorcycle accident in the rain. The question of suicide threaded through the words, unasked, as the article revealed that Mr. Graham struggled to cope with his sister's murder, three years prior. On the next page, *DNA Analysis Links More Victims to Serial Killer John Darcy,* along with a photo array of twelve girls. In small print, a list of names started: *Likely victims include Janine Graham, previously reported as a runaway.* Mr. Graham's sister was the girl in the top left square. In the picture, too, she reminded me of Brynn.

Mr. Graham was the only suicide I'd seen. Remembering something Mr. Cooper had said to me, I flipped through the book, searching for other teachers.

The next teacher who caught my eye was Miss Andersen. A cold chill ran down my spine: *Poison Peggy Found Dead,* her headline blared. The article read, *Peggy Andersen was found dead in her home Tuesday morning of apparent natural causes. Andersen had been awaiting trial for the murder of her sister, Beatrix. Andersen famously answered, "Just a little," when police asked if she'd poisoned her sister.*

I looked up. "Mr. Cooper was trying to tell me something that night at the dance, wasn't he?" Charon didn't bother to answer, and I was already flipping through the book. Dr. Falzone's article was easy to miss. Guess they didn't allot too much page space for drunks who drove into a car full of teenagers and later died of cirrhosis. I remembered how Dr. Falzone had squeezed my shoulder after I'd gotten in trouble, and how he'd come looking for me the morning Jessie disappeared. It was hard to believe his old life had been so full of despair.

"Have all the teachers killed someone?" I asked.

Charon paused before answering. "For teachers, the requirements to obtain a coin are more stringent. In the past, they proactively intervened to change fate, usually by taking a life. They unbalanced the universe with their actions. To leave Lethe, they must repay what they have taken. They must help students cross, but they must not proactively interfere. As psychopomps, they are required to wait until the right set of circumstances allows them to pay their debts."

I shook my head. "I don't understand."

"During his life, Henry Graham suffered survivor's guilt, believing he did not deserve to live while his sister was dead. Eventually, his mind twisted until he thought his own death could pay his sister's coin; that to sacrifice himself, he could retroactively save her."

"That's why he couldn't take Brynn's coin."

"Yes. He must not pay for anyone's life but his own. Mr. Graham's penance was not only to stand by as students passed, but to help one go. As it happened, you were the one. He could help because you asked."

I thought of Mr. Graham, what it must have taken out of him to deliver me into the hands of death. I wished I could go back and tell him I was OK.

Unlike most of the other obituaries, Mr. Cooper's disappearance and presumed death were discussed on a glossy magazine page, apparently a national interest story. Our drama teacher had been spelunking in a New Mexico cave. His whole party had gotten disoriented deep below the earth. "Our compasses may have malfunctioned due to a geologic anomaly — a large portion of metal ore nearby," one of the surviving explorers was quoted as saying. "But I can't think of any cause for the lanterns to fade in and out." *Against the advice of the group, spelunker Gregg Ross rappelled into a crevasse. When he did not reappear, George Cooper followed to assist. Minutes later, both returned. "I'll be right back,"* Mr. Cooper *was reported to have said, as he went back into the crevasse alone. He was never seen again. His rope was retrieved, severed. For twenty-four hours, firefighters, policemen, and volunteers attempted search and rescue. No member of the rescue team reported compass or light malfunction. Mr. Cooper was never located. When interviewed, Mr. Ross was unable to recall any detail of the spelunking trip.*

"Mr. Cooper's different," I said. Charon nodded. "He helps people figure out they're dead, doesn't he?" I asked. "I saw him on your boat in one of the pictures."

Charon shrugged. "Yes, he is unlike the others. Cooper is my assistant. Long ago, he made a pact with another, and this put him out of my grasp. Over time, he has seen the error of his agreement. Now he watches the others as they learn and go, hoping to find a way for himself."

"Another?" I asked, but Charon did not answer. Dread, like ice water, trickled down my spine as I considered what kind of supernatural creatures could be waiting in the cracks of the earth for an unlucky traveler. What creature could cheat death? What price had Mr. Cooper paid? I turned the page.

Nora Alpert. Nora had been brushing her teeth when a weak spot in an artery blew like a bald tire. My friend had been dead before her body had hit the ground, her awesome brain drowned in blood. Her coin-collecting dad pounded at the door, but her body blocked it closed. That was why she'd been so set on locking the secret room.

The brain obscures the events of death, Charon had told me. Maybe part of Nora believed she'd locked that bathroom door, instead of dying against it, like Jessie, who believed she'd buckled her seat belt. Suddenly, I remembered the day of Brynn's egging, how horrified Nora had been. "The door's locked," she'd said about the balcony doors. But then she'd changed to say, "It's blocked." Had seeing Brynn trapped behind that door helped Nora start to figure it out, then?

I touched her obituary and missed her like crazy. Nora's whole life was so short there on the page, not at all saying how cool she was, how her runner's legs had been so strong they had taken her wherever she needed to go. I blew my nose. *Good-bye, Nora, I'll miss you*, I thought.

The next obituary was one of those weekend edition articles. It had a photograph of a swollen and frail girl in a hospital bed, surrounded by family and flowers. My fingers felt cold on the paper, and I remembered what Charon had said. "Usually, by the time a person meets with me, they have completely passed." I pointed at the book. "She's not dead."

I guess Charon didn't need to peer over to see who I was talking about. He said, "She is here but not dead."

The first article was a request for donations. The family's oldest daughter had died of illness, the article said, and a few months later, their younger daughter was diagnosed with the same disease.

"She's going to fight it," her father was quoted as saying.

The next article about her: *Hope Remains Strong for Family of Illness-Struck Girl.*

Then: *Local Charity Raises 100K for Treatment of Ten-Year-Old Tamara Stratford.*

The next one: *Valiant Efforts Fade as Girl Slips into Coma.*

From a magazine, instead of a paper: *Right-to-Life Battle Wages in Small Town.* It read:

The marriage between Todd and Penny Stratford survived the devastating illness and death of their oldest daughter. But just three years later, their other child was diagnosed with the same severe form of the disease. When twelve-year-old Tamara suffered a massive stroke as a complication of treatment and fell into a coma sixteen months ago, the Stratfords' tattered union dissolved.

Since their separation, the Stratfords have not come to an agreement on the continuation of their daughter's life support. The father's lawyer states, "Doctors have determined Tammy has no hope for recovery. Any movement or behavior she exhibits now is only reflexive—the misfiring of damaged circuits in her brain. To keep her on life support dishonors the active and loving child she once was. Her father wants peace for her."

The mother's lawyer states, "Tammy responds to light and the sound of her mother's voice. She smiles and she makes noise. Tammy may not have the type of life the rest of us do, but that does not give anyone the right to end it."

The two quotes were separated by a grainy black-and-white photo of my roommate. Not the snarky girl I knew, but pale and slack-faced, bald in spots from rubbing against her pillows. By chance or not, the photographer had caught a glimmer of a smile on Tamara's face as she lay there, surrounded by family.

"How is she here if she's also there?" I asked.

"She is both places and neither. More like a weekend visitor than a full-time resident in either life. She fights to live. But there is not much for her in that hospital bed. She comes here to grow and learn as a normal child would."

I glanced down at the picture again. Two teenage boys sat on the empty hospital bed next to Tamara's. They were identified in the print as her cousins.

"They were in my room." I jabbed my finger at one of the boys. "She told me they weren't, but they were."

"The reality around Tamara is warped. What you saw that night were living boys bleeding through into our world. Just as when you sat too close to Tamara, you perceived the hospital and her illness, the vortex into her other world. It made you sick. It makes her sick as well. She smells death on you."

Ew. I didn't want to smell like death. I gave my pit a discreet sniff. I didn't smell anything. Still, I felt bad. I thought about the night I had hugged Tamara, the antiseptic smell floating around her.

"Will she die?" I asked. Charon didn't reply. After a moment I realized the answer. Of course. Everyone dies.

CHAPTER 24

The next page was mine. I knew before I even read it. The article was no more or less ordinary than any other I had seen: *Minor in Grave Condition After Pool Party Tragedy.* Below, it read: *Police and EMS were summoned to 113 Peacock Circle at nine o'clock yesterday evening in response to a drowning. Reports indicate horseplay resulted in the victim being pushed into the Jacuzzi, where her long hair was drawn into the drain, trapping her underwater. Rescue and resuscitation efforts were performed by minors in attendance. The victim was transported to Community Hospital and is listed in grave condition. Drug use or foul play do not appear to be factors, although a toxicology report is pending.*

For a moment, I am there again. *". . . go swimming," she says. The shove knocks the wind out of me. I spy the first star in the sky. Then bubbles in the water. The hard scrape against my butt as I hit the underwater bench, and still I'm falling. Water up my nose . . .*

On the next page I saw: *Camden Fisher, fourteen, died Monday due to complications from a near drowning earlier this month. Services will be held at Goode & Sons on Thursday, from ten to noon.*

You might think seeing that kind of thing would be a terrible shock. But it wasn't. It was like part of me that was suffocating could breathe again. At least once I knew the truth, I could go from there. I had drowned. My funeral was on a weekday.

Sitting in the gold-and-navy-striped club chair, I opened my mouth. Instead of words, a gush of water spilled out. It was the weirdest thing — not like throwing up, when your stomach muscles get all sprung. It was my lungs squeezing the water up and out. I tried to shut the book in my lap, horrified I'd ruin it. Well, as much as a person can be horrified while she is coughing up Jacuzzi water. It spilled all over my obituary. And disappeared. Ghost water, I guessed. The pages stayed dry. I gagged up another waterfall. I should have known better than to think Charon would try and help me or anything. He stared over my head, out the window, at the black sea and moonlight.

When my lungs were clear, they stung something awful. And then it was like I was really breathing. Like somehow, I had been walking around with pneumonia or half a lung without even knowing it. I took a deep breath and laughed. I guess I was high from the extra oxygen. I thought: *This must be what newborn babies feel like, getting air for the first time. I always thought they were crying, but I bet if it's like this, then they're trying to laugh.* Everything smelled a thousand times wonderful.

And then something made me want to start bawling all over again. It was the smell of my mother. I looked all around, expecting to see her. There was no one but me and the boatman.

"My mom told me I didn't have to go if I didn't want to." Even though I was sitting there in that comfy club chair at sea level, everything inside me was also standing at the open door of an airplane. I was in that moment before you jump out and slip into weightlessness, right before you cannonball into gravity. *Do I have a parachute?* All this time, Charon had been leading me to the edge, and now here I was, pinwheeling my arms and not able to scream because everything inside of me knew that this was what I came for. I closed my eyes and fell.

It was a memory. The first thing I saw were my mom's hands on a brown storage box. I was home, packing for school. Except it wasn't exactly a memory at all, because the box wasn't in my room. It was on a hospital bed. And I was in the bed, and there was something in my mouth and all the way down my throat. I waited for my mom to show me that dorky picture of me and Lia. The only thing I heard was the mechanical hiss of a ventilator. The memory of sitting in my room with my mom, packing for boarding school, got peeled apart and I saw what had happened.

My mother had brought the box to my bedside during the week I had been between dead and alive. It was full of my old stuff — pictures, that teddy bear my dad had won at the fair for me. I had never told her about my airplane dream. Instead, she'd brushed my hair and held my hand and I said nothing at all.

And then something happened. First, machines started to beep, all irregular and alarmlike. Then the sharp squeak of nurse shoes on the floor. I tried to concentrate on the warmth of my mom's hand on mine, but it felt like I was floating away from her.

My whole arm smarted like a bee sting. The feeling crawled up to my shoulder and into my chest. Everything went bright-colored flowers behind my eyelids, and my heart thumped hard. The beeping got steady. After a while,

I could hear the slow squeak of nurse shoes departing. Until at last only my mom was still there, holding my hand. I tried to squeeze back. In my mind's eye, I could see her sitting next to me. She looked like a vacuum and I had tripped over her cord and unplugged her from the wall. *This is just a dream*, I wanted to tell her right away. Anything to make her feel better. She stared down at the carpet, the way she did when she had lots of things on her mind and was trying to figure out which one she wanted to say.

Mom scooched her chair close to the bed so she could put her forehead on my forehead, and she brushed my hair with her fingers. I heard her sniffle, and felt her tears on my cheeks. I could smell the good mom smell of her. It made my scared feelings go away. I wanted to tell her how much I loved her.

The monitors started to beep again, urgent and erratic and far away. My mom whispered in my ear, "Well, Camden. You don't have to go if you really don't want to."

And that's how we both knew I was going for sure.

It was still night when I woke up. Charon was gone, and there was an old quilt thrown over me. My eyes were crusty and swollen, but it felt like all the tears were out of me. My spine popped from the small of my back all the way up to my neck when I sat up. I wrapped the quilt around me and stepped out of the building onto the dock. Charon stood in the moonlight. He turned to me and every little cell in my body suddenly wanted to jump off the dock and swim away. *Little late there, survival reflex*, I thought. *Where were you in the Jacuzzi?*

"So what happens now?" I asked.

"Do you have passage?" he asked.

I felt in my pocket for the gold coin. "Yeah."

When he turned back to me, his face was terrifying and skeletal. "It is time for you to fulfill your requirement. Think on everything I have shown you, and make your visitation."

I shivered. "What if I can't? I mean, if I'm not ready?" I asked.

Even though he was a little bit away from me, it felt like he was also right there, breathing on my skin. I got the crazy idea that he was barely restraining himself, like in a moment, he would cross the distance and grab me up against his old-paper body and suck the soul right out of my body, ship or no ship, ready or not. He didn't, though.

Instead, he said completely the opposite of what I expected. "You may go back to school if you feel you have more to learn. I can make it so you do not remember that you are dead. You will rediscover it eventually and experience this night again. Some of your classmates have chosen to do this instead of crossing. A few have done so many times."

He said the last so casually that I wondered if maybe I had already been here and chosen to forget. I could not imagine wanting to ever do this again.

There was an old pay phone against the wall of the clubhouse, and I knew what I was supposed to do, but I couldn't move.

"I can't," I said. "I don't know what to say."

He said, "This is not for you. It is for her."

As soon as I put the phone to my ear, the line started ringing. It rang and rang. A gentle wind blew in my face, salty and damp.

"Hello?" Lia asked, over the phone line. Hearing her voice was like getting punched right in the nose. My eyes stung and my head was full of stars. There were a million things I wanted to say. They logjammed in my head.

I guess she knew it was me, though, because she started bawling. My cheeks felt cold and I realized I was crying, too.

"Hi," I said.

"You're not really here," she said. "I'm making you up."

"That's funny," I said, into the phone. "I was thinking the same thing about you."

She laughed and sniffled, all together, like it was one thing. "I waited so long, and nothing. I thought if . . ." Her voice broke. "You would come back and let me know it was OK. You know. After."

I thought about all those times I'd wanted to call her and had been angry instead, and when I'd called her and listened to her breathe on the other end of the line.

"I got here as quick as I could," I said.

"Tell me something. Like a message that I couldn't make up on my own, so I know it's you."

I thought about it. Then I said, "The summer we were ten, we dressed your dog up in your old baby clothes, put him in a stroller, and walked him around the neighborhood." I choked up.

"I hate you!" Lia yelled into the phone. I guess she must have believed it was me then. "How could you die on me? You ruined my life!"

"*I* ruined *your* life?" It was all that I could do not to hang up. She was alive. And I was in a strange place, away from my family and friends, dead. All because of her. Who did she think she was?

"I'm the girl who killed my best friend!" she screamed.

The first star in the sky. Then the bubbles in the water. The hard scrape against my butt as I hit the underwater bench, and still I'm falling. Water up my nose. The back of my head hits bottom. Ouch. I try to flail my way to the surface, but something down here yanks me back.

"My hair got caught," I whispered, running my hand through what was left on my head. Not a sleek little bob at all, but hacked and ripped out of my scalp, by the feel of it. "The drain?" How many times had Lia and I tickled our toes on the suction there? *Up there in the breathable air of the end-of-summer party, they are still laughing. I thrash my legs and pull at my hair, but I'm caught. Lia's legs plunge in. She yanks my arm. "Ouch," I try to tell her, but I can't. Her hands grope down over my face, into my hair where it connects to the drain. Through the water, I can hear her yelling, screaming, "Something's wrong. Turn off the power!"*

More legs splash in, churning up so many bubbles I can almost breathe down here. They yank me, but still, I'm stuck. Kevin starts bailing water out with his two cupped hands, like he thinks he's gonna empty the Jacuzzi before I drown down here. Somebody's knee comes down on my stomach and I puke air bubbles. Reflexively, I gasp, and when that chlorinated water comes in, it stings. I cough it out, but my stupid lungs keep sucking it back in. I'm drowning, I think. Where's Lia? The worst is she's not in the Jacuzzi anymore. How could she leave me like this?

And then there's a huge splash. "MOVE!" Lia shouts. She plunges a big, serrated knife through the water. I know what it's for. It's to cut cake, after hamburgers.

What's she doing? *I'm not cake, I think. Everything is weirdly funny, and the need to breathe has passed. I must be a mermaid. Lia's down here with me now, too, and in the water, her face is crumpled in sobs.* Hey, don't cry, *I try to say.*

And then my best friend takes the knife to the back of my head and starts sawing my hair. It feels like my head is a giant, wiggly tooth. She has to go up once, twice, to breathe. The last strands pop, and I am free, coming up, in Lia's arms. And when I break the surface, everyone is screaming.

"You saved me," I whispered into the phone.

"No, I didn't." Her voice sounds like she was the one who drowned. "You died anyway."

I held the phone to my ear and said, "Dork, you totally did. It was the water that got me."

"I don't hate you," she whispered, after a few moments.

"I knew that," I said. Lia laughed and sobbed, like she was stuck inside an emotion blender, and all the things I loved about her were coming through the phone line as soup. My heart swelled up like a new bruise to hear them. When she was done, I listened to her breathe. It felt good to hear the *ticktock* of her body.

"Tell me something else about us," she said. "You know, some secret."

The wind shifted and the waves lapped against the dock posts under my feet.

"I had a secret crush on Kevin Meyers," I said out loud before I even thought it.

It surprised a laugh out of her. "I knew that," she said, echoing my tone. Then she sobbed like I had stepped on her fingers until the bones broke, but that wasn't the worst. The worst was that her voice was getting faint, like someone was turning the volume down. I pressed the phone hard against my ear. "You were worth a million of that guy. I'm so sorry."

I knew what she'd done. One stupid, impulsive thing.

She'd also been my best friend since second grade. "I forgive you, on one condition."

"Anything," she said.

I thought about Mark, still stuck back at school. It felt like my chest opened up and the wild bird that'd been trapped inside flew out, free. I said, "You have to forgive yourself. You have to let me go."

"I can't." She wailed.

"I know who you are," I said. "Promise me." For a long time, it was only the sound of her crying, and I was scared for her.

But at last she said, "OK," and I knew by her promise it would be.

There were a billion more things I wanted to tell her, but the phone was getting more static with every second. I said, "Tell my parents I'm safe and good. Tell them, I'm . . . um . . . I'm graduating." I was shouting into the phone.

From very far away, I heard Lia say, "I'm graduating, too." It stole my heart out of my chest. In real time, in alive time, had all of high school passed? I was going to miss Lia's whole life.

In the last few seconds that I knew she was on the line, I searched my head like mad to give her something good. I finally realized there was only one thing I had to say. "I love you," I yelled.

Faintly, I heard her say, "Love you, too."

And then she was gone.

For a while after, I stood on the dock, thinking about all the things I wished I'd said to her. Who was Lia now, if she was old enough to graduate? Not a fourteen-year-old with a killer smile anymore. That girl was as much of a ghost as I was. But even so, Lia was out there, somewhere, still my best friend.

"What's on the other side?" I asked Charon.

"I have never stepped on the other shore," he answered.

"Yeah, but you know something about it, I bet."

Eventually he said, "Consider an unhatched chick. That creature believes the entire world is the inside of an egg. Then things begin to change. One day, there is no more nourishment, no more room. I find it hard to imagine a more frightened creature, with nowhere to go and no ability to stay. That small bird must put its head against the edge of the world and break through its own reality in order to continue on. And yet, this happens every day. If the universe has such an elaborate plan for a chicken, perhaps one could hope there is also a plan for you."

In my pocket, I held the coin until it was warm in my hand. I listened to water lap against the dock posts. Behind us, the first streaks of purplish dawn appeared. Perhaps it was a warning — a sign that lightness was behind me and darkness ahead. Or maybe it was just the sunrise. I shivered from the cold, even though my body should no longer care about things like that.

What about everyone I loved? What about the good smell of my mom when she hugged me? What about the sound of my dad's voice? What about Mark? Nora? Lia? Would I ever find them again if I went across the water?

You do, a voice inside me whispered. *You do see everyone again.*

Charon waited with me. The streaks of dawn in the sky remained, unchanging. My heart started up with the pitter-patter racing of happy fear.

See, I knew what was on *this* side. But over there, across the water? Anything could be waiting, as different from this dark place as the bright light of day compared to the inside of an egg. I took a deep breath, taking my time. You know. Considering.

ACKNOWLEDGMENTS

For a long time, I was afraid to write. I worried people wouldn't like what I had to say. That fear seems kind of silly to me now, but it felt very real when I started. The cure, of course, was to write anyway. As I did, I came to realize I was surrounded by all kinds of amazing mentors. Which was really lucky for me, since I'm a big chicken on my own. I'd like to thank the following people for helping me understand it's OK to be scared, as long as I don't let fear get in the way.

A heartfelt thank you to Charlie, Karen, Peg, Mary, Carol, and especially Kari, all of whom read what I wrote and sometimes didn't like what I had to say. How wonderful to learn it wouldn't kill me! Most of the time, it even helped. Thank you for your insight, clever suggestions, and encouragement.

A huge thank you to Cori Stern. My dad used to say, "If something seems too good to be true, it probably is." Cori has been the exception to this rule, being both way too good to be true, and also everything she claims. She, along with the incredible Bruna Papandrea, helped make publication possible.

On the publication end, I'd like to thank my agent, Eddie Gamarra, who has been fantastic. I am also hugely appreciative of the Scholastic team. Many thanks to Yaffa Jaskoll, who created the beautiful book design; Janet Robbins, the production editor; and Becky Shapiro.

I couldn't have asked for a better editor than Aimee Friedman. She saw how to make my manuscript about ten times better, and was incredibly kind, deft, and insightful about sharing that information with me. She put a ton of energy and thought into this project, and has remained enthusiastic about it since the very first. It has been a privilege to work with her.

Much love to my father, who believed I'd be a writer long before I did, and to my mother, whose brilliant understanding of character helped me when I had no idea what to do next. Finally, to my children and husband, who gave me the space and encouragement to try this. Change can be frightening, especially when it occurs in a parent or spouse. But they are brave, amazing individuals, who helped me become something more than I was before. Thank you.

As a teenager, ANNE APPLEGATE attended boarding school near Santa Barbara. She later graduated from Tufts University with a degree in psychology, and now lives in California with her husband and three children. You can visit her online at www.anneapplegate.com.